TALES OF THE WESTERN TRAIL

TALES OF THE WESTERN TRAIL

WHITE COUNTY CREATIVE WRITERS

THORNDIKE PRESS
A part of Gale, a Cengage Company

GALE
A Cengage Company

LIBRARY OF CONGRESS CIP DATA ON FILE.
CATALOGUING IN PUBLICATION FOR THIS BOOK
IS AVAILABLE FROM THE LIBRARY OF CONGRESS.

ISBN-13: 978-1-4205-1476-6 (softcover alk. paper)

Published in 2024 by arrangement with Kimberly Vernon.

Printed in the USA
1 2 3 4 5   28 27 26 25 24

The White County Creative Writers' Club
has provided invaluable education,
assistance, and encouragement to each
of the authors contained in this collection.

Gary L. Breezeel, Del Garrett,
Don Money, Rhonda Roberts,
Gary Rodgers, Kimberly Vernon,
Ellen E. Withers, Anthony Wood

KEEPING A PROMISE

BY ELLEN E. WITHERS

Numb, Abraham Powell had walked for weeks. A road-floured Texas Sharpshooter uniform hung on his gaunt six-foot frame. The soles of his boots were razor thin, but he felt lucky to have them. They only needed to last a bit longer. One more stop before heading home. Much as he wanted to cut and run, he'd promised.

He left Texas to fight for a Southern nation assembled from independent states. At his return, his dreams were reduced to ashes and the lost cause responsible for dirt mounds over thousands of men.

When the sun peeked over the tops of the cedar trees, he realized it was noon. A finger of the Sulphur River shone in the light and brightened his path, proof he must be close.

He reached a lane described to him long ago. A five- or six-year-old girl skipped down the road to greet him. As she neared, the eyes of his best friend looked out at him from her smiling face. With one glance into those warm, brown eyes, Abraham knew he'd arrived.

The urge was strong to turn his head skyward and shout, 'Henry, you live through the eyes of your daughter.' Instead, while crouched low, he said, "You must be Henrietta."

She drew back a little. "Do I know you, mister?"

He shrugged his bedroll, his haversack, and his satchel onto the dry Texas soil. "No, but your Papa and I were soldiers together."

"My Papa died in the war," she said.

He nodded, not trusting his voice.

"What's your name, mister?" She eyed his torn gray trousers.

"Abraham."

She sucked in her breath and a dimple appeared in her cheek. "I know you! Papa wrote about you."

"He did?"

"You're here to see Mama."

Her words stung him — no, he had a promise to keep.

"I'm here to see you and your mama."

She jumped up and down. "I'll take you to her."

His spirits rose when he picked up his load to follow her, and she danced in the dirt around him. Once ready, he took her hand. It felt soft and small against his callused palm.

She led the way to a simple wooden house near the top of a gently sloping hill. At the yard, she skipped ahead. Her single black braid swayed as she ran to a woman on the porch with needlework on her lap.

After a moment of conversation, the figure stood and clung to the porch rails as he approached. She wore a pale blue dress, clean but worn. Locks of straw-colored hair were twisted into a bun, yet a few untamed ringlets curled around her temples and neck. Her eyes matched her dress, blue and worn.

He read the sad look on her face. Couldn't blame her one whit for wishing it was Henry standing in front of her instead of him. He wished the same.

The bags hit the dirt again. His boots clunked onto the porch and he transferred his forage cap from head to hand.

"Abraham," she said and extended her hand. "Thank you for coming."

Her voice was a song to his ear; a tune and timbre seldom heard during the past few years.

"Mrs. Hale." He took her hand in his. "A pleasure meeting you, ma'am."

"Please call me Sarah. Won't you sit down, sir?" She made a sweeping gesture to the chair on the porch and picked up the darning tossed aside at his arrival. "Of course you must stay for dinner."

"Please don't go to no trouble."

"It'll be my pleasure." Then she disappeared into the house.

Henrietta tugged on his trouser leg.

"Is Abraham your calling name or your other name?"

A grin escaped while he considered her question. "My last name is Powell, but please call me Abraham."

She pointed to the chair. "Mama said for you to sit down."

"We must do what Mama says." With a wink, he sat down.

She sat on the porch facing him, her dress spread around her in a pale yellow circle.

"Where are you from, Mister Abraham?"

"I was born and raised in Texas."

"Just like me! Where have you been?"

"Your Papa and I fought in Louisiana and Arkansas. Then . . . ah, I mustered out in Indian Territory."

Her eyes narrowed in seriousness. "Were you shot like Papa?"

"I was. Took a musket ball in my shoulder."

10

"My Papa died from being shot."

"Yes, he did." He laced his fingers together, keeping his eyes on his hands. Silence filled the space between them.

"Won't you tell me about the Indians?"

"Of course. Did you know the boys play a game with a ball and sticks?"

"Do girls get to play?"

"Can't say for sure. Girls were mostly with their mothers, preparing food or keeping squirrels out of the cornfields. The Choctaw are farmers, like us."

"We don't raise corn now. Mama said we can't plant nothing needing more than a hoe for seeding."

He stood and walked to the edge of the porch to scan the property. Part of the barn roof was gone. The fence missed several boards along its length. The rectangular fields were covered in weeds, not near ready for spring planting.

Why did Henry's widow continue to work this land? No way she'd ever manage to farm it. She should move to town and forget about this dirt.

Henrietta broke into his thoughts with another tug on his trousers. "Want to see the barn?"

"How 'bout a tour after dinner?"

Sarah called from the door. "Almost

ready. You want to wash up?"

Henrietta led the way to the well. He filled the bucket with cool water while she dug in a nearby wooden box until she filled her fist with a bar of soap. A smile split his face, anticipating the long-denied luxury of being clean. After she washed her hands, he lathered his arms, neck, face, and hair.

She giggled at his actions. "Are you taking a bath?"

"Henrietta, a few weeks ago, I went to a bathhouse. They boiled my clothes and my bedroll, while I bathed and shaved. I was covered in dirt and crawled with critters."

"Crawled with critters?"

"Soldiers suffer from lots of things we can't control. Most of us had measles early on, and then we fought stomach upset. Once the lice came, they never left."

"What's lice?"

"Tiny bugs that crawl on your skin."

She scrunched her face. "You mean like ants?"

"Yes, but smaller."

She shivered and cut her eyes toward him. "You don't have any more critters riding with you now, do you?"

Laughter burst forth, foreign to his ears. "No, I left 'em back in Ft. Smith."

Inside, a fine cloth and three sets of dainty

cups and saucers were spread across the table. Thick slices of bread, toasted and stacked high onto a platter, sat beside a butter dish and jam jar. Three bowls of soup steamed from their places on the table.

"Oh Mama, we're gonna use the company cups! And have jam, too!" Henrietta clapped her hands in glee.

When Sarah smiled at her daughter, Abraham spotted redness in her eyes. Tears were expected from a young widow who grieved for her lover. Was his visit worth the burden of making her relive her pain anew? The shame of his actions swept over him.

Henrietta chatted happily throughout the meal. She relayed his Indian tales to Sarah without notice of her mother's eyes. Did she often see her this way?

Once finished, Henrietta ran outside to get water for washing the dishes. With her occupied, he could speak freely.

"I didn't mean to come here and cause you pain without reason." His face warmed. Then he rose and the screech of his chair on the wooden floor filled the silence of the room.

On the porch, he dug inside his haversack and found the bundle of letters tied with string, then the gold watch, cold to his touch. The last of the items, a small red

13

leather journal, finished the pile of gifts.

At the house's threshold, he saw Henrietta at the well. One day, these objects he held in his hands would be hers. Would she ever know the essence of the man he'd called friend?

Inside, he placed the journal, the watch, and the bundle of letters in front of Sarah. At the sight of them, her eyes flew wide and erupted with fresh tears.

"Your Henry was the best friend a man could have. We fought side by side until I took a bullet in my shoulder. When they told me he'd been killed, I was laid up, but I was able to find him and get his personal things. His watch and journal were with him all the time, the letters in his bedroll. I can't read very well, but I believe they're all addressed to you."

She held the journal against her wet cheek. In her other hand, she clutched his watch and letters.

"I promised Henry I'd give these to you . . . if something happened." He spun on his boot heel and headed toward the door.

In a voice brimming with emotion, she said, "Thank you for bringing these to me."

He nodded and went out the door. Henrietta was at the edge of the porch with the bucket, so he stepped quickly and took it from her. "We can go exploring now."

He set the bucket beside the door and prayed the thud of his boots on the porch would muffle the sobs coming from the house.

To give Sarah the time she needed to grieve, he and Henrietta covered every square inch of the property. While the child chattered, he fought to keep his mind off Sarah and her broken heart.

That evening, Henrietta fell asleep in the rocking chair with him. He carried her to the loft, then he and Sarah remained in the chairs, watching the colorful flames dance in the hearth.

"Henrietta has fallen in love with you."

He nodded, running his upper teeth over his sun crusted lower lip. "I've fallen for her, too."

He let the peace of the moment flow over him. The crackle of the fire brought to mind the eternity that had passed since he'd enjoyed the pleasure of a fire, the company of a beautiful woman, and a rocking chair.

"I'm so glad to have Henrietta. She's the image of her father, isn't she?"

"She is. She's also like him in spirit."

"You noticed that, too?"

He took a deep breath. The tension

drained from him as he basked in the tranquility of the evening. The only sounds filling the room were squeaks from the rocking chairs and an occasional pop from the fire. Never again would he suffer through the burst of artillery or screams of dying men.

"Henry thought highly of you, Abraham."

"Yes. With bullets flying 'round your head, you grab aholt of friendship when you find it. He liked everyone in the regiment, but there was something special between us. We were like brothers."

"He wrote that you were like me — quiet, reliable, and loyal."

He considered her words while they rocked in comfortable serenity.

She broke the silence. "What are your plans now?"

"I'm headed home. Figured I'd work in my uncle's tannery. It's a smelly job, but it's what I know." Then he plunged ahead with a question of his own. "Why haven't you moved away from here, Miss Sarah? You and Henrietta deserve a better life than the one you've been living."

She rocked in silence for so long he figured he'd offended her, or she was too much of a lady to answer. He was surprised when she spoke.

"I may be able to do that now . . . now that you brought back all of Henry that'll return to me."

She faced him. "This place was all I had of him, other than his baby. After he died, it was a way to hold on to a piece of him."

"I understand," he said, and meant it. Being a man who'd lost a war and left hope buried in the battlefield cemetery beside his best friend, who would better understand her desire to cling to a memory? After fulfilling his promise to Henry, what did he have to hold on to?

She pulled a handkerchief from the pocket of her dress and dabbed her eyes. "I have a proposition. Take tonight to think it over."

He nodded.

She looked at the flames. "Only Yankees have money around here. I'd rather starve than sell this land to one of them. I'm left with a farm I can't handle and no way to let it go."

At her pained expression, he stopped rocking. What was she about to say?

"Would you buy this farm from me?"

His eyes darted to the floor. "I don't have that kind of money, Miss Sarah."

"You could work the farm and pay me over time with the produce. It would let me keep food on the table and put aside a little dowry for Henrietta."

His heart hammered in his chest. A fine piece of land he could one day claim as his own. His own slice of Texas. He'd have no reason to leave it behind again.

She twirled her handkerchief in her lap. "You're a Texan and were my husband's best friend. Who better to claim his birthright?"

His stomach tightened. Henry's birthright, passed to his widow and child.

She stood. "You'll let me know your decision tomorrow?

"Yes. Good evening, ma'am."

He let himself out the door and to the barn. Accustomed to sleeping under a blanket of stars, he improvised a straw bed, covered it with his bedroll and situated it under the hole in the barn roof. The canopy of Texas stars held his attention for a long time before sleep crept in to join him.

At sunrise, with an ax conscripted from the barn, he worked on a supply of kindling for Sarah. The physical exertion helped settle a mind that had whirled with indecision since her suggestion last night.

Henrietta ran up with a small basket tucked under her arm. "I'm gathering eggs for a fine breakfast. Won't it be a pleasurable way to start your day?"

Before he could answer, she ran off to complete her chore.

He was again reminded of how much she favored Henry. Like him, she found happiness in every part of life. Could her spirit save two people crippled by loss?

When he returned to splitting wood, he realized hope wasn't buried with Henry after all. Instead, hope had followed him to his best friend's birthright and shined from the face of his child.

THE FASTEST GUN

BY DEL GARRETT

It doesn't take much effort to kill a man. Skin your hog leg out of a low-hung, tied-down holster, aim it like you're pointing your finger, and pull back on the trigger.

The gun does all the work, giving you that satisfying loud bang and puff of blue smoke coming from the end of the barrel when you fire it. All you have to do is beat the other guy to the draw and have guts enough to live with seeing a man get killed, knowing it was you who did him in.

Trace Meadow wore his Colt .45 low on his hip and tied down tight. He sported a new smooth-leather holster with matching cartridge belt and a silver concho on the holster's cross strap. Trace looked the part, all right, but he was no gunfighter; truth is, he'd never killed anything bigger than a jackrabbit.

But he wanted to.

He'd bought his gun rig when he turned

seventeen. He spent every penny he'd earned shoveling out horse droppings at D.L. Meacham's cattle ranch in Alta Loma, Texas. He rode an old plug that D.L. had given him and he slept in the hayloft above the horse stalls. He ate what he could find as a handout and sometimes washed dishes at the Alta Loma Café for a few pennies and a full meal.

He was a skinny kid, of course, and because of his stable work, he smelled like horse dung, so he wasn't the most popular citizen in town. Folks said that was what made him so unsociable. That wasn't it at all. Trace wanted to be like everyone else, but being dirt poor and wearing dirty rags on his rail-thin frame, his appearance didn't help him any with the ladies. Only the town's stray dogs seemed to like him, maybe for the way he smelled, or just because he didn't object too much when they occasionally used one of his legs to relieve themselves.

Over the years, the boy's constant rejection by the townsfolk developed into a finely honed fit of hatred and disdain for the citizens — those who dressed nice and ate well — and he especially fixated on the cowboys his age who had no problem courting the young ladies in town. He daydreamed a lot about goading those fancy dans into a gunfight and him whipping out his pistola like Wyatt Earp or even Butch Cassidy and showing them all who was boss of the fast draw.

Trace had only one redeeming factor. Once a month he strolled down to Meacham's creek that divided the sand bar in back of the big house and jumped in, clothes and all, and scrubbed himself down with a bar of lye soap. He'd come out of the quiet stream all rinsed off and sit on the creek bank with a fishing pole in his hand, waiting for the hot sun to dry him out. A bath, catfish for his supper, and ten cents in his pocket, he'd ride to the Horseshoe Saloon in town for his once-a-month mug of warm beer, his only affordable vice.

Tonight, he had the unfortunate luck to bump into Billy Rice, spilling his beer on the older boy. Billy had a good-natured temperament most of the time, but tonight he'd had a few beers too many and had tossed them back as chasers for the whiskey he'd been drinking.

Billy also worked as a cow-puncher for D.L. Meacham and had a knack for bulldogging and branding. His work made him strong and D.L. paid his men well. It just happened that tonight Trace bumped into

Billy when Billy was well into his liquor and getting low on his money.

"Hey, you piece of horse piss, watch who you're bumping into!" Billy shouted.

Trace didn't need any more encouragement to let his temper fly, so he slid a few choice words out of the side of his mouth and Billy was still sober enough to realize he'd been insulted. He grabbed Trace by the collar and threw him up against a support post, causing Trace to drop his mug. He'd only gotten two sips out of it before bumping into Billy, and he wouldn't have any additional beer money for another month. It was going to be a long, dry spell, and that made him mad enough to take a swing at the cause of all his troubles.

A bad mistake, because Billy, being a good size bigger, was known to be good with his fists, so he landed a few hard punches that instantly caused Trace's eyes to swell up, both with tears and a large amount of puffy redness.

Everyone laughed, of course, and their laughter stung Trace more than Billy's fists had done.

Trace backed out of the saloon, spouting a string of cuss words while Billy just stood there laughing at him, along with everyone else in the saloon. Alta Loma had no real entertainment, so any squabble like this was cause to pause and cheer on the winner.

Somebody bought Billy another beer and one of the barroom beauties sidled up to him to enjoy his company, knowing Billy was generous to the ladies. Billy passed the free beer to her and ordered a shot of tangle-leg rotgut instead.

Meanwhile, Trace had made his way back to the hayloft where he slept and dug out his shiny new holster and six-gun. He'd never worn it except when he was alone. He kept it hidden under a pile of hay under his ragged old army blanket he called his bed.

Tonight, he was mad enough to strap the belt around his waist and slick back the pistol like he'd read about in the dime novels of the day. Tales of gunfights and derring-do have always thrilled young boys and mostly all of them lived vicariously through the adventures in those books, only a few like Billy the Kid or Mysterious Dave Mather or Wes Hardin ever lived the hard life for real.

Tonight was going to be Trace Meadow's time of reckoning.

"I'm fast, Billy," he said. "Faster than you, for sure."

Billy Rice represented all the wrong things that had ever happened to Trace, all the depression in his soul, all the embarrassment of a lifetime of being a nobody with nothing in his pockets but ten cents once a month and no respect from anybody. All that, while the 'Billies' of the world lived it up high on the hog.

"They're gonna respect me tonight," Trace growled.

His hand slapped leather and the Colt .45 flew into his palm like it was made just for him. He repeated the fast draw three more times before pausing to load cartridges into the gun's cylinder.

Back at the bar, the piano player pumped out a lively rendition of Camptown Races, then softened the keys while one of the more talented soiled doves sang a Jenny Lind love song. She slurred the last note when she saw Trace Meadow barge through the bat-wing doors and head straight for Billy Rice.

"Billy Rice! You son-of-a . . ." Trace already had his pistol in his hand before Billy dropped his whiskey glass and went for his own gun. The other cowboys in the Horseshoe dove for the nearest pillar or post, scooting chairs and tables across the floor as they went. Poker chips crashed to the floor. Beer and whiskey glasses flew across the room. Hats sailed through the air. Bar girls scrambled away like fast-fleeing hoppity-toads. Only the bartender remained motionless, transfixed by the happenings, unable to take his gaze off the two young men who now stood only six feet apart.

Trace raised his gun another inch, not quite in line with Billy's chest. The room echoed the sound of two rounds exploding. Blue-gray smoke filled the air between the two of them and Trace's brow furrowed, taking in the sight of Billy's unstained shirt. He saw the smoke wagon in Billy's hand and knew he hadn't yet pulled his own trigger on the cowboy. Looking down, he saw two black powder holes burned side by side in his ragged denim shirt and knew he'd been hit.

He didn't feel the pain at first, just some pressure on his chest like somebody had struck him with a sledgehammer. He stumbled back and fell to his knees, looking at the shock on Billy's face. The ranch hand held his gun on Trace, following the boy's retched body as he fell to the floor, coughing up blood.

"Why'd ya do that, Trace?" Billy screamed, his hand starting to shake. "I didn't want to shoot ya. I ain't never killed a man before. Why'd ya do that?"

Trace didn't answer. His thoughts raced

back to all the dime novels he'd read, remembering all the stories he'd heard of all the high-noon shootouts, and he wondered how it was that all his life he never wanted anything except to be accepted by the people he'd met. If he couldn't be respected as a person, he'd settle for their fear of him as a gunfighter. This was supposed to be his night, his rise to fame.

He closed his eyes and dipped forward in the pool of blood that now built up underneath his body. His finger still on the trigger, he belched up a gurgling chuckle as he gave in to the darkness surrounding him.

"Wow! You sure are a fast draw, Billy." The bartender shook his head in awe and admiration and went back to polishing a whiskey glass as the piano man jingled the ivories to the tune, Get Along Home, Cindy.

Billy didn't say a word. He just sadly thought to himself, it doesn't take much to kill a man, all you have to do is beat him to the draw. The gun does all the work.

No Courage in a Bottle

BY GARY RODGERS

"Stay out of our way, you stupid half-wit. Real men don't hang around begging for a drink." Laughter from Jackson and his friends followed.

The words echoed through my mind as my shoulders hit the hard-packed earth in front of the saloon and I rolled against the legs of a horse. Using the horse's leg, I pulled myself to my knees. A dark rage boiled in my gut, but I knew I was defenseless against the men standing on the boardwalk. As the horse sidestepped away from me, I heard an unfamiliar voice speaking. It was the horse's rider.

"Don't you fellows think that's enough?"

Jackson and one of his hands started off the steps, but stopped when the man spoke. Looking up, I didn't recognize the stranger, and as good as it felt to have someone speak up for me, I wanted to tell him not to get involved. Yet something about his eyes told

28

me to stay quiet. Then I noticed a man whispering to Jackson and pointing behind the stranger.

Struggling to my feet, I looked where the man was pointing. The stranger was leading two other horses with bodies tied across the saddles. In this part of the territory, that usually meant one of two things. The man on the horse was a lawman, or a bounty hunter. Either way, Jackson and his crew wouldn't be happy with the stranger interfering in their fun.

Jackson made a motion for one of his men to look at the bodies tied across the saddles, then turned back to the stranger.

"Mister, you need to keep on riding and mind your own damn business. Cory here," nodding toward me, "is the town drunk. We can keep him in line without you butting in. Unless you'd rather take his place and us have a little fun with you?"

A few of the men laughed at their boss's remarks as he smiled at the stranger, but Conner, Jackson's brother, stepped forward and whispered in his brother's ear. The smile disappeared from Jackson's face as he stared at the stranger and a different mood settled over the situation.

I glanced up at the stranger and, for the first time, I noticed a small double-barrel shotgun resting against the saddle horn. Without having to look, I knew he was aiming it at Jackson.

"Boss, one of these fellows is that half-breed, Blue Eyes. The other one is Wiley Mayes. They're dead, Boss."

Eyeing the stranger, Jackson asked, "Just who are you? And why are those men dead?"

The stranger looked the men over before answering. Something in me made me move to the far side of his horse. Being unarmed, I wasn't willing to be caught in a showdown. All I wanted was whiskey. You can't find that if you're six feet under.

"Grump Stokes. And I have papers on both men. Chances are, I have papers on some of you men, or could find papers at the marshal's office. So, unless you intend to join those men, I suggest you let this one-armed man here take my horses to the marshal's office." He held the lead rope to the other horses out for me to take. "Then I can buy him a drink and get back on the trail."

With the offer to buy me a drink, I snatched the lead rope from his hand and started down the street. It would take me out of the line of fire for one, and if gunplay didn't ensue, I could earn myself that drink

I was looking for. I might be the town drunk, but I'm not stupid.

"What if I told you those men were friends of mine?" Jackson began. "Would that . . ."

Conner interrupted Jackson and whispered something to him again, keeping his eye on Stokes as he did.

Jackson stepped back on the boardwalk before speaking again.

"You go on with Cory and take care of your business. If you want to buy him a drink after, fine. But do it somewhere besides here. We don't need your kind in here."

Spinning on his heel, he hurried through the saloon door, followed by his hands. I continued up the street, glancing back in case Jackson or some of his men came back out. Stokes was eyeing me, but not once did he look back as he followed me to the marshal's office. I guess he figured my reaction would tell him if any of them came back out.

At the marshal's office, I tied the lead rope to the hitch rail and took a seat on the boardwalk. I had little interest in what Stokes' business might be, but I wasn't going anywhere till I got that drink. Marshal Lewis must have heard us outside, because he came walking out as Stokes dismounted to tie his horse.

"Cory, what have you got here? You haven't gone and killed someone, have you?" The marshal asked jokingly.

"No Sir, Marshal Lewis. This fellow stopped Jackson and his men from giving me a hard time down at Charlie's place. I was just trying to get a drink out of them. But he offered to buy me a drink if I would lead his horses down here."

"Grump Stokes, Marshal. I've got papers on these two. If I can collect my money, I'll be on my way. After I get Cory that drink I promised." He pulled some wanted posters out of his vest pocket as he spoke.

"I've heard of you, Mr. Stokes. You're that bounty hunter from Texas, ain't you?" It was more of a statement than a question, as he took the papers and walked out to look at the men tied across the saddles.

"That's right. The Judge up in Ft. Smith sent word asking me to help in the territory. I've got a letter here saying your office is one place I should work with."

"You mean one of the places to collect your bounty," the marshal said as he walked over to look at the men tied to the horses. "I don't reckon I've ever heard of any bounty hunters looking to work with the law. But I can get you paid. These fellows match the papers you have. Can't say anybody will miss them either. Unless it's that bunch Jackson Wyatt and his brother have got working for them. I wouldn't mind seeing some papers issued on that sorry bunch. Cory, lead those horses over to Pete's and come on back."

I gathered the lead rope and shuffled my feet a little. If I went to Pete's and he got started talking, Stokes might leave without me getting that drink he promised. I wanted to say something, but knew the impression it would make. Stokes must have read my mind.

"It's okay, Cory. I'll be here when you get back. I want to see what other posters the marshal has hanging up. While you're at it, bring that roan back with you, and the guns off that half-breed. I might still have use of those."

"Yes Sir, Mr. Stokes." I would have tried to carry that horse back if it meant getting that drink.

At the stables, Pete was full of questions I didn't have answers for. I knew how to be polite. Pete hired me from time to time to clean out the stables or fix some fence. And he let me keep a bedroll in the loft, so I had a place to sleep. I didn't want to mess that up. He didn't pay me much, but it allowed me some grub and an occasional drink. Lately there had been more drink than grub. I wasn't proud of it, but it dulled the pain some.

Besides running the livery, Pete was the acting town undertaker. I helped get the dead men off the horses and stripped the gun belt off like Stokes had asked. Pete objected until I let him know I was told to bring the roan and the guns back with me.

Leading the horse back to the marshal's office, I could see both men waiting outside the office talking. I was ready for that drink, so I hoped they had little to talk about.

"Cory, I agreed to go down to Charlie's with you and Mr. Stokes. He said he promised you a drink and figures if I'm with you, those Wyatts won't be near as eager to start trouble. I couldn't swear to that, but it would probably be best if I'm there."

His scowl told me he had rather not go along. To be honest, I didn't want to either. But I wanted a drink, and Charlie's is the only place to get one if Stokes didn't have a bottle in his saddlebags. I had been hoping he did. I started to tie the roan to the rail when Stokes stopped me.

"Bring that horse with you, Cory. I might have a business proposition for you. If you're interested, you'll need a horse."

I followed behind the marshal and Stokes a short distance. Even with the two of them, I wasn't eager to have another run in with the Wyatt brothers. I'd gotten used to them roughing me up once in a while. But after the earlier encounter with Stokes, I suspected they'd want to make an example out of me. I cursed myself for being the way I was. I hadn't always feared a fight. But whiskey changes a man, and I needed a drink worse than anything right now.

I was still several steps behind Stokes when he walked through the door. The silence coming from inside told me they had been expecting him. I followed the marshal in, not quite certain what to expect. But I meant to have me a drink. I wasn't prepared for what came next.

I was close on the marshal's heels as we entered the saloon. Stokes had already made it to the bar, and I could see most of the crowd had their eyes on him. Jackson had risen from his seat at a table and started as if to move toward Stokes when the marshal spoke up.

"Keep your seat there, Jackson. Mr. Stokes is here to buy Cory a drink and be on his way. So, you and your boys let them be, and I won't have to lock any of you up today."

"Marshal, I done told Mr. Stokes he

needed to do his drinking somewhere else, or there would be trouble. Now you don't want to go and make me out to be a liar in front of all the folks, do you?" Jackson laughed.

"They can think of you as a liar, or a coward," Stokes interrupted. "One ain't much better than the other in my book. But unless you keep your seat like the marshal asked, they'll be putting your name on a marker in whatever passes for Boot Hill in these parts."

Jackson stopped in his tracks, unsure of what move to make next. I could see three whiskeys on the bar beside Stokes and knew what my next move would be. While they glared at each other, I hurried over to the bar and took one and downed it fast. I meant to get out of there before any gunplay started.

"Easy there, Cory. We have some business to discuss." Stokes held my arm as I turned to leave. "Here, let me fasten this gunbelt on you. A man doesn't need to go around a town like this unarmed."

I hadn't noticed Stokes carrying the half-breed's gunbelt in with him. But I stood motionless, maybe terrified, as he fastened the belt around my waist and tied the holster around my leg.

"There you go, Cory. How does that feel? You will find having a gun on your waist keeps cowards like Jackson from kicking you around and making fun of you." He could see my hands shaking and winked. "But I think you already knew that, didn't you?"

I hadn't worn a gun since coming home from the war. When they released me from the prisoner camp, I weighed a hundred pounds, and all the fight was gone out of me. When I made it home to find my wife and daughter had died of smallpox, I turned to the bottle and never looked back. It surprised me to find comfort in having the gun on my side.

"Marshal, you need to move out of the way. I've had enough of this drygulcher calling me names and challenging me in front of my men." Jackson was on his feet, glaring at Stokes.

"Stokes, he has a point. You've been goading him ever since you walked in here. I can show you and Cory outside and watch you ride out of town. No guarantee they won't follow you. Or I can move out of the way and let you and Jackson settle this right here." The marshal's eyes said he was hoping it would be the former.

"Jackson, what if I told you I bet Cory here could take you?" Stokes was glaring at

Jackson now. "Would you be more willing to fight your own fight instead of having your men back you up?"

"I, I, I'm no gunfighter," I stammered. "Are you trying to get me killed?"

Jackson's laughter struck a nerve in me. "You want me to kill this drunk, so you don't have to buy his drinks? I can do that. But then I'm killing you too."

Stokes turned to face me and spoke. "I can handle him if you want, Cory. But the man who lost his arm on the battlefield in Kentucky doesn't need another man to fight his battles." He smiled at my reaction. "That's right, I recognized you when I first saw you in the street. I can tell you more, but only if you're willing to ride with me and learn to be the man you once were."

The confidence in his eyes was something I used to see in my own. I could walk out of the saloon and continue to be a drunk, or I could take a chance on being killed on the spot.

"Perhaps it's time I became a man again," I answered.

Stokes stepped out of the line of fire as I focused on Jackson Wyatt, sweat beads forming on my forehead.

"Okay, Cory. You want to die, I'll be happy . . ." his hand streaked to his pistol.

Too slow.

It happened too fast for me to think about it, but now my hands were shaking. Holstering the pistol, I reached for a shot of whiskey on the bar, but Stokes' hand covered it.

"You can turn back to drinking, Cory, or you can join me on the trail. I owe it to you for pulling me off the battlefield. Even if we were on opposite sides. But if you go with me, the drinking stops."

I eyed the whiskey as Stokes moved his hand away, desperately wanting to down the brown liquid I had grown accustomed to using as my crutch, but the idea of finding the man I used to be sounded good.

"Mr. Stokes, I think I would like the chance to be a man again. I might be hell to live with for a while, but I think you already knew that."

"Call me Grump. Now let's go find some food and get started finding the man I met in the war."

LOVE THY NEIGHBOR

BY GARY L. BREEZEEL

Yancey Colburn sat astride Goldie, his palomino gelding, atop the ridge and surveyed the land below. Rich in grass and other vegetation, Verdant Valley certainly lived up to its name. In the distance lay the settlement of New Hope. "Well, Old Pard, we're almost there. A new place not devastated by war where we can make a fresh start."

Below and to his right, a horse burst into view at a dead run. A slender young female hung onto its back as if for dear life. It must be running away with her. With a gentle kick, he urged Goldie into motion and set a course to intercept.

Moments later, they overtook the runaway, and Yancey pulled the victim to safety. As his mount slowed to a walk, three riders flashed past.

The girl twisted in his arms and slugged his shoulder. An odd way to show gratitude for saving her life.

Fire blazed from her eyes. "What are you doing, you . . . Oh, I don't know what to call you. I had the race won. You made me lose."

"Sorry, Miss. I thought your horse was out of control."

"Put. Me. Down. You brute." She wriggled and squirmed.

He lowered the wildcat to the ground and caught his first real look at her. Luscious chestnut curls flowed around her shoulders. Cute upturned nose. Slender, shapely figure undisguised by her plaid flannel shirt and tight jeans. Gorgeous, even when red-faced with fury.

With chin held high and feet wide apart, she glared. "Now, catch my horse and bring him here. If it's not too much to ask."

"Um . . . yes, ma'am." At a click of Yancey's tongue, Goldie leaped into action.

He found the stallion grazing beyond a bend a quarter-mile down the road. Yancey grabbed the reins and led the animal back to its owner.

"Thank you." She accepted the reins and mounted up. "Now, it's my fervent wish never to see you again. *Goodbye.*" She spurred her mount to a gallop.

Yancey chuckled. What a woman! Such

41

fire. The man who won her would never have a dull moment, but he'd soured his chances from the start.

An hour later, he rode into New Hope. He'd visit the blacksmith before he left town. Goldie had a loose shoe. But first, he needed to locate the land office. Ah, there it was on the right. He pulled to a stop, tied the gelding to the hitching post, and strode through the open door.

A bald man with a green eyeshade looked up from a stack of documents. "May I help you?"

Yancey removed his hat. "I hope so. Can you tell me how to find the Goodwin ranch?"

"A waste of your time. Old Roscoe Goodwin died last month."

"I figured as much. His letter said he didn't have long to live." Yancey drew a paper from inside his Stetson. "Before I forget, can you tell me where to have this deed recorded?"

The land agent took the document and opened it. His eyebrows rose. "Why, this is a deed to Roscoe's ranch." He chuckled. "My, won't this stir up a hornet's nest."

"What do you mean?"

"You'll see. Once word gets around. For sure cussedness, that gal's got a Missouri mule beat, hands down." He slapped his knee. "Oh, the county seat's twenty miles straight along this road through town. You'll have no trouble finding the courthouse." The man left his chair and strode to a map mounted on the wall. "Here, let me show you how to find your spread."

The sun had risen high in the sky by the time Yancey awoke the next morning, He'd worked long into the night to make the house habitable. The place had gotten rundown during Roscoe's illness. Today, he'd tackle the barn. He stretched and hopped to his feet. Time for a late breakfast. He shuffled through the parlor on his way to the kitchen.

Someone pounded on the door. "Open up, you scalawag. I know you're in there."

What in the world? He crossed the room and opened the door. The girl he'd "rescued" stood on the porch, her face as red as the day before. Her nostrils flared. She clenched and unclenched her fists. "How dare you come here with a phony deed and steal this property out from under me!"

"The deed's valid. I haven't stolen anything."

She stamped her foot. "I will *not* let some confounded stranger swoop in here and destroy my life. Who do you think you are?"

"I'm Yancey Colburn. Roscoe Goodwin was my father's best friend. They grew up together. Both fought with Sam Houston. Roscoe disapproved of his no-account nephew. Said he'd sell the place and waste the money on corn liquor. So, he deeded his ranch to me. Livestock included. I'm sorry if this interferes with your plans, Miss . . ."

"Hollis . . . Millie. I own the spread to the south. Okay, if you're the owner, I'll buy it from *you*. Same terms I offered Elliot — five thousand cash."

He shook his head. "It's not for sale."

"I need this land. My cattle will die without water. I'll lose everything my parents poured their hearts and sweat into for twenty years."

"I like it here. This ranch is my chance for a new start. I can't give it up."

She turned on her heel and stomped off.

A week later, Yancey knocked on Millie's door.

She opened it, dishtowel in hand. "Yes?"

"I have a proposition for you."

Her eyes lit up.

"Hold on. I haven't changed my mind."

Her shoulders drooped. "Might as well

come in." She led the way into the parlor, pointed toward a chair, and took a seat opposite. "What's your idea?"

"Before we discuss that, I'm curious. What have you done for water up to now?"

"A branch of the creek ran through our spread. Spring fed. Flowed without interruption even in dry spells. Until this April. Now we get a trickle for a day or two after a rain. Nothing more."

He tugged an ear. "That's odd."

"No kidding."

"Have you tracked it upstream?"

"As far as my east boundary. Ellsworth Mumford has his property posted. Threatens to shoot trespassers. Has a half-dozen hired guns."

"Sounds suspicious. I'll bet he's offered to buy your ranch."

"Right. For fifteen cents on the dollar."

"I take it you suspect he's dammed the branch to starve you out and acquire your place cheap."

"Bullseye."

"Listen, I've looked my ranch over. I have enough water for your herd and mine. I'll give you access while we figure out how to solve your problem."

Her head snapped back. "You'd do that for me?"

"We're neighbors. Why not?"

The corners of her mouth ticked up. "Perhaps, I misjudged you."

As Yancey strolled into the mercantile, an elderly lady stepped away from the counter, basket in hand. "Thank you, Mr. Hooper. See you next week."

The storekeeper pulled out a card, wrote on it, and returned it to its place. Then he faced Yancey. "May I help you?"

"I have a list of supplies here." He handed it over. "Oh, do you carry sorghum molasses?"

"I do."

"Add a container to my order. I'll pick it up in an hour."

As he turned to leave, a tall, heavy-browed man with dark hair silvered at the temples strode to the counter. "Hooper, have you received my shipment from Chicago?"

"Not yet, Mr. Mumford." The storekeeper twisted his hands together.

"What's the holdup?"

"I-I don't know. I'll telegraph the supplier and inquire."

"You do that." The rancher whirled around and stormed out.

So, that was Millie's nemesis. Arrogant and overbearing. A formidable foe, indeed.

46

■ ■ ■ ■

After a month on his new place, Yancey rounded up the last of his cattle and drove them into the west pasture. Less than eight hundred head, a far cry from the two thousand Roscoe claimed in his letter. A degree of attrition due to months of neglect was natural. Some may have escaped and mixed with nearby herds, but most had probably fallen victim to rustlers. No doubt, many now populated Mumford's range. Still, he'd found sufficient high-quality stock to serve as the foundation of a strong herd.

He stared at the creek. With no rain for two weeks, the stream wouldn't stay full enough to maintain both his and Millie's cattle for long. They needed to solve her water problem. Soon. Which meant he'd better figure out a way to learn what had gone wrong. But how?

Yancey arose at midnight, dressed in dark clothes, and headed for the barn where he saddled and mounted Goldie. The half-moon provided sufficient illumination to find his way. He rode across Millie's ranch to the branch and turned upstream. Once he neared the boundary, he dismounted and dropped the reins. He descended into the streambed and followed it onto Mumford's property.

After about an hour, a barrier blocked his progress. In the shadows, he couldn't tell what it was. So, he climbed. Made of earth, the obstruction slanted toward the top. When he reached the peak, the silver moon reflected off a wide expanse of water. Mumford had dammed the stream . . . but what could they do about it?

"Hey, you!" An angry voice shouted. "What do you think you're doing?"

Uh-oh. Better make tracks.

As he turned to flee, gunshots rang out. Fire burned through his left side. He slid down the dam and sprinted downstream until he discovered a gap between the trees that lined the streambed, then he pivoted and raced across a field toward a stand of timber. Maybe he could lose them there.

When he'd caught his breath, Yancey plunged into the woods. Brush rustled not far away. They'd gained on him. He climbed a nearby tree and hunkered down till his pursuers passed. After an hour, he scrambled to the ground and crept away. He'd have to take a roundabout route home to avoid detection.

He stumbled onto the porch at Millie's

ranch as dawn broke. Blood soaked his shirt. He knocked on the door. And collapsed.

Yancey awoke in a soft bed covered by a colorful patchwork quilt. Where was he?

"You're awake."

He turned his head to the right. Millie sat in a chair beside the bed, embroidery in hand.

Now he remembered. His explorations the night before. The injury. He pulled down the covers.

She grabbed his hand. "No need to check. The bullet just grooved your side. I cleaned and bandaged the wound. You lost some blood, but you'll be fine. How'd you manage to get yourself shot?"

"I snuck onto Mumford's ranch to find out what happened to your water."

"I told you they'd shoot trespassers on sight." She wet her lips. "Did you discover anything?"

"Sure did. He's got an earthen dam. Good-sized reservoir."

"The scoundrel. It's illegal to obstruct a stream in Colorado."

"Let's go to the county seat and bring the sheriff."

She shook her head. "No point. Mumford

owns him."

"Then we'll have to take care of it our-selves. I ran across a half-full cask of black powder in my barn. Enough to do the job."

"Yeah, but since he knows someone dis-covered his dam, he'll double his guards."

"With a good diversion to distract his hired guns, I think I can make it."

"Be careful. It's sweet of you to take my problems on yourself, but I couldn't stand it if you got hurt worse because of me."

"I dislike bullies. I do whatever I can to ensure that they get their comeuppance. But I'll need your help."

A cloud blocked the sun as Yancey waited on Millie's place near the property line two days later. *Hope it's not an omen.* He checked his watch. One fifty-eight. In two minutes, she and her ranch hands would approach the entrance to Mumford's acre-age and demand to talk to him about the dam. With luck, he wouldn't expect a daylight raid, and the uproar would draw his guards to the other side of the spread.

Time to make his move. Yancey tossed the saddlebags containing the fuse over his shoulder and tucked the cask of powder under one arm. He jogged as fast as he could along the route he'd taken two nights earlier. His eyes darted left and right as he searched for any sign of Mumford's gunhands.

Twenty minutes later, he arrived at the dam. With his knife, he dug a hole a foot deep halfway up the embankment, inserted the powder, and attached a fuse. But as he reached for a match, a gunshot rang out. The bullet kicked up dust a hairbreadth from where he knelt.

He stretched out prone on the ground and drew his six-gun. Rifle in hand, a yahoo peeked from behind a wagon a hundred yards away. Yancey snapped a shot in the gunman's direction. Although his Colt wasn't accurate at this distance, it might make the guy think twice about leaving his cover.

No way he could stay here. The shots would bring the other gunslingers. Yancey crawled toward the streambed. When he reached the bottom, he ran for the nearest tree. More gunshots sounded. Once under cover, he returned fire at the shooter who now stood atop the dam.

While he watched, two men joined the first. One started down the embankment. If Yancey didn't act now, the whole plan would fail, he'd die, and Millie would lose her ranch.

He had one slim chance. He propped his wrist on a low branch, took careful aim, and squeezed the trigger. Dust kicked up three inches too high. After a slight adjustment, he fired again.

Boom! The man at the foot of the dam flew ten feet toward Yancey and lay still. The other two disappeared in the blast.

Best get to higher ground. Any second, water would burst through here with a vengeance. He scrambled up the bank and sprinted for the woods. Thank goodness he was on the opposite side of the torrent from Mumford's killers.

When he reached Millie's ranch house half an hour later, she stood beside the now placid stream that flowed past, a silly smile on her face. As he approached, she turned, ran to Yancey, threw her arms around him, and pressed her lips to his. After a moment, she pulled away. "I can't believe you did this for me. After how I treated you."

"The Bible says, 'Love thy neighbor.' "

"I'm not sure this is what Jesus had in mind, but I'll take it."

He touched her cheek. "I had to do it. When you lit into me that first day, I knew you were the one for me. So much fire. I'll never tame you, but I want to spend the next fifty years trying."

"Is this some kind of left-handed proposal?"

He scratched his head. "I reckon it is."

"Then, the answer's *Yes.* You risked your life to help me. You're a man of integrity. Someone I can count on."

"Are you sure you don't want to marry me just to get my ranch?"

She glanced at him with a coy expression. "Maybe . . . but after the church bell rings, you'll have a lifetime to figure it out." She planted another kiss on his lips, one that took his breath away.

Yancey grinned. *What a pistol! She'll keep me on my toes.*

Counted Not Among the Dead

BY ANTHONY WOOD

"My sister's in there! Get her out! Please!" Men and women rushed from every direction to make a water bucket line as the volunteer firemen ran their wagon too close to the flames. They fell back from the heat, choking and coughing from inhaling heavy smoke. A loud crack. An ear-splitting pop. The cupola gave way and crashed into the center of the burning ruins of the Marion County, Mississippi, courthouse.

Ashes of all the important papers — land deeds, censuses, birth and marriage records — floated up into the night sky like so many lightning bugs in summertime. The recorded life of families who pioneered our county vanished in a blue hot blaze. It was all by design. Big leather books smoldered in the ashes, along with my Uncle Silas. And with him, my big sister, Marion.

I cried. I screamed. I finally fainted into the arms of the volunteer firemen who held me back. The sheriff was addressing the crowd when I woke. Not a stick of the courthouse was left standing.

"The war's been over, but carpetbaggers and scalawags have been burnin' down courthouses everywhere. No account men with no breeding who steal good folk's property while the government turns a blind eye. Sadly, we lost more than our county's records tonight. Two of our fine citizens died in the fire — Mexican War veteran Silas Tullos and his lovely niece Marion. Silas guarded our courthouse every night. His last words when I saw him earlier tonight were, 'I fought at San Jacinto with Gen'l Sam Houston, and I'll keep them thievin' carpetbaggers away!' I've got a good idea who caused this calamity. I'll be leadin' a posse come first light."

Truth be told, the sheriff didn't know who'd done it. I didn't, either, and I didn't know what to do, not until I heard a whisper when I stepped into Uncle Silas's old house at the edge of town where we lived.

"Sissy, that you?"

I shrunk back, never having seen a ghost before. I squeaked out, "Yeah."

"It's me, Marion."

"You're alive!" I hugged her and didn't want to let go. She finally peeled me from her body.

"Anyone think I'm alive?"

"No, they think you burned up with Uncle Silas with nothing left to bury."

"Good. Then I can do what needs doin'. You can't charge a woman with a crime if she's dead. When it's done, we'll come back. I won't be counted among the dead."

"Sheriff's leading a posse in the morning."

"Does he know who did it?"

"Do you?"

Marion didn't say, but she knew — a preacher, a voodoo witch, and the ringleader — a beady-eyed carpetbagger who you knew lay awake every night scheming like the Good Book says.

"When are you leaving?"

"Soon as I get packed."

"I'll be coming with you."

"Good. Throw some bacon and beans in a flour sack. I want to get a jump on the posse."

We sneaked west out of town smelling of smoke — and vengeance.

Sleet pelted Marion's face like buckshot, but she didn't flinch. No unexpected early spring ice storm could stop her.

"They ain't gettin' away with it. Not by a

long shot. I'll catch 'em come hell or high water. I'd just soon go ahead and catch hell first, then get baptized again in the Mississippi River on the way back through — whether I need it or not." She let out a little chuckle — a rare event.

"You'll catch hell all right. That pistol toting carpetbagger is no fancy pants dandy dude. Aren't you scared?"

"I'm more scared of what I'll do when I find that low down skunk. Besides, they won't be expectin' me. I'm dead, remember?"

"For what you're planning, you better get them sins washed off. If we make it back, that is. You do know a preacher has to do the dunking or it won't take."

"No scalawag preacher is ever gonna touch me again. Besides, the Bible never says who has to do the immersin'."

Marion read her Bible religiously and could hold her own arguing scripture with any preacher foolish enough to try her on. I wouldn't dare, even though I had more schooling.

Marion sniffed. "Ol' preacher took up with that voodoo witch when I worked in Natchez. I know where they're headed."

"Where?"

"To Hell after I'm done with them, but

west to the Indian Territory first. Out there, outlaws who want to get lost won't be found. They won't get that far, though."

My horse shivered and snorted, shaking the ice from her mane.

Marion patted her horse's neck. "Ain't that somethin'? A scalawag preacher, voodoo witch, and a thievin' Yankee carpet bagger conspiring to burn down the county courthouse to get rich. Beats anything I've ever seen!"

I shivered worse than my horse. "I can't believe Uncle Silas is gone. They don't make them any better."

"Ole witch tried to kill him just before he went to work at the courthouse last night. Took the little pension money he'd squirreled away in a snuff jar and left her pet cottonmouth in his bed."

"No! I thought she came just to help out an old veteran, keeping house and such."

"And offerin' a little "comfort" now and again. I warned him, but he wouldn't listen. He did yesterday afternoon though, when her cottonmouth's fang caught his thumb. It swelled up bigger'n a cucumber. 'Don't hurt so bad,' he said, when I brought his supper to the courthouse. Those were the last words he ever spoke to me." Marion wiped a tear. "That snakebite won't go unanswered."

Her name was Marion. I don't know if they named my big sister after the county when Ma and Pa came to Lott's Bluff or if the county was named after her. History is often written by those who spin the best fairytales. Either way, she had the spirit of the Swamp Fox they now claimed inspired the name. She was the prettiest girl in the county — too pretty to stay in the orphanage they put us in when our folks died.

Marion sneaked to my bed one night. "I'll come back." She slipped away into the darkness. I had no idea where she went. Not until Uncle Silas came for us when he moved to Mississippi from Georgia. That seems so long ago.

"How do you do that?"

"Do what?"

"Go on like you're not freezing your hind end off."

Marion said nothing. Cold blustery wind never seemed to bother her. Nothing did. My hair was frozen to my hat.

Marion muttered under her breath, "Hadn't been for Uncle Silas snatchin' me up by the hair of my head and gettin' me out of that 'den of iniquity' in Natchez, I'd already be counted among the dead."

"I didn't know, honest I didn't."

"Some things you do because it's the right thing to do. Some things you do because you don't have a choice. And some things you choose to do to make a wrong right."

"Uncle Silas saved you?"

"Wasn't like a knight in shinin' armor in some storybook, if that's what you're thinkin'. He knifed a man to get me out of there. Then he came for you. Said he couldn't leave you with a child-violatin' preacher in that orphanage. No more'n he left me to rot in Natchez."

"He wasn't our real uncle, was he?"

"Closest thing to an uncle we'll ever have. Pa saved his life in the war. Guess Uncle Silas was payin' him back by takin' care of us." A tear sparkled on her cheek. "He taught me how to be human again." She brushed away the tear. "Now hush up! I'm tired of talkin'."

Marion didn't mean anything by her harsh words. She had a good heart. Working in a house of ill repute made her hard. Uncle Silas murdered made her dangerous. The only sweetness she had left was in what she was doing now — avenging Uncle Silas's death and caring for me. There'd be no sweetness though, when she caught up to his killers.

We reached the Homochitto River as the sleet let up — but the cold didn't.

"Aren't we taking the ferry?"

"Strip down to your drawers. Now!"

I tied my clothes to my horse's saddle. "I can't swim very well."

"Great, then I'll have four deaths on my head."

I had nothing to say to that.

Marion waded out into the swollen current and yelled, "Grab your mare's tail and follow me. I've got her reins."

Midway across, my hands slipped. I yelled, but there was nothing Marion could do. I crawled out on the sandy bank a quarter mile downstream and limped my way up-river.

"Why didn't you come after me?"

"You're here now."

"I could've drowned!"

"I taught you how to swim, didn't I?"

"Yeah."

"Then there it is. Knew you'd make it. Besides, I knew you'd need a fire when you got here. Get under this tarp and strip off them wet rags. Take this blanket I've been warmin' for you."

I thought my teeth would chatter right out of my head. The blanket and fire felt good, but not my feelings. It wasn't Marion's fault I was swept away. Neither was Uncle Silas's death her fault, or Ma's and Pa's, for that matter. But she took it that way.

I didn't know how to start, but I did. "Marion?" She didn't look up from drying off two shiny pistols. I didn't ask where she got them.

"Yeah?"

"When will you stop taking responsibility for things not yours? Those robbers killed Ma and Pa, not you."

"I might as well have. I hid, too scared to move. They butchered Ma and Pa. I'll never get that out of my head."

"You were only seven."

"Old enough to pull a trigger!"

"Going after Uncle Silas's killers won't fix that."

Marion handed me a steaming cup of coffee. "No, I can't fix that. But I will fix this." She threw a stick on the fire. "Enough! Put on these old work clothes. We don't want to be seen as two women traveling alone. Open a can of beans and then get some rest. I want to make the Rodney ferry tomorrow before dark. We leave before daylight."

■ ■ ■ ■

The sun set in the west as we crossed the Mississippi River. The ferryman said three ragged characters traveling fast crossed not four hours earlier. Marion handed him an extra dollar.

At dusk, we sneaked up to the edge of a nothing little Louisiana town named Waterproof. The ferryman told us a steamboat captain named the place when he saw an early settler standing on the last piece of dry ground surrounded by floodwaters — hence, Waterproof.

I expected fire and brimstone to rain down from heaven any minute for the wickedness I saw there — drunks lying in the street, scantily clad women calling after every man, and gamblers looking to separate anyone from his money.

"I didn't know such places existed."

Marion snickered like one of Satan's minions. "You've never been to Natchez, have you?"

I understood then, Marion knew how to fight evil — become more evil than the demons she wanted dead.

The town proper seemed deserted except for the fancy wooden building lit up at the other end of the muddy street. Men brandishing shotguns guarded the doors.

Marion pointed. "There. Let's hide the horses around back." She handed me a pistol. "When I say shoot, you shoot, but not before."

No one noticed us with our hats pulled down when we took a table in a corner. It was that kind of place. A large pit commanded the center of the room and men placed bets as women caressed their bodies, hoping to cash in on some of their winnings. Marion and I peeked over into the pit. Several rattlesnakes hissed, angry at being poked.

A crusty old timer holding up a silver dollar cackled, "Here comes the Voodoo Queen!"

She swung her hips from side to side, carrying a caged raccoon high in the air.

"Place your bets, boys. My 'coon against five deadly serpents." The carpetbagger took bets as the scalawag preacher counted money.

Marion whispered, "Stay here. Fire every bullet you got when I say."

I felt for the pistol as Marion made her way around the ring.

The voodoo witch's eyes rolled up into the back of her head. "May the gods of my ancestors fill this masked warrior with power to defeat Satan's slithering dragons."

Just as the voodoo witch opened the raccoon's cage, Marion shoved her into the pit. Rattlers latched onto her from every angle. She screamed. Marion shoved the flailing raccoon into the carpetbagger's face. He flopped around on the floor, his eyes torn from their sockets. The preacher ran to the bat wings with Marion hard on his heels.

Just before she exited, Marion smashed a coal oil lamp in the corner where the carpetbagger lay moaning and yelled, "Shoot!"

I fired every round I had into the ceiling. I ducked through the smoky blaze and scrambling crowd after Marion. The carpetbagger ran out of the saloon covered in flames, clawing at his eyes. I gasped for air, looking for Marion. She was holding the preacher's head underwater in a horse trough across the street.

"Touch me again, will you, preacher?" She let him up for a breath. "Any last words?"

"Please, I ain't ready to die! I need to repent!"

"No time left for repentin'! This baptism will just have to do!" Marion held him under until no more bubbles came up. "In the name of the Father, Son, and the Holy

Ghost, I say, amen!" She let go and collapsed.

I threw a double handful of water on her face and she jumped up, ready to fight.

"It's done, Marion. Let's go."

In the noise and confusion of the fire, we walked our horses out of town unnoticed back to the ferry and camped for the night.

The deed was done, but absolution was in short supply. We crossed the easy flowing big muddy river at sunrise.

A young preacher stood on a stump near water's edge speaking words of mercy and grace to a small crowd.

"Ain't nothin' you've done too long, or too bad, that God won't forgive your every wrong."

Marion handed me her reins and hopped off her horse. She looked up at the preacher. "Is it true? What you're sayin?"

"Every word."

"Then I'm ready."

The preacher hurled himself into the air, arms raised to heaven. "Hallelujah! Witness God resurrect this soul from a grave of sin and give her new life!"

Marion shucked her boots and walked into the silty stream, holding the preacher's hand. She turned and smiled at me for the first time in a long time.

"Told you I wouldn't be counted among the dead."

*"Counted Not Among the Dead" was published in the Winter 2021 *Saddlebag Dispatches.*

THE BOUNTY HUNTER'S REWARD

BY KIMBERLY VERNON

Boyd Watts strode across the dusty street, squinting against the afternoon sun. His boots pulled toward the Silver Nickel at the end of the street, but he fought the urge and continued to the mercantile. The last job had been a long one, through rough country, and he'd depleted all his supplies. With that bounty in his pocket, he needed to restock before he allowed himself to visit the saloon.

When he pushed the door of the mercantile, it bumped into a young woman, causing her to drop her basket. "Pardon me. I am so sorry. Let me help." He bent to retrieve her parcels.

"Excuse me," she said, the color rising in her cheeks. "I wasn't watching where I was going."

Boyd looked up and got lost in the most beautiful green eyes he'd ever seen. His tongue turned to dust, and no words came.

He scrambled to his feet and handed her the basket and its contents. He snatched his hat from his head and mumbled, "Ma'am," though he barely recognized the squeak as his own voice.

He stared after her as she hurried out of sight. That was no saloon girl, he was sure of it. He'd never seen such a lovely lady, and he sure hoped he'd run into her again. He smiled at his own play on words before allowing the door to close.

"Can I help you, Mister?"

The shop keeper's words jarred him back to the moment, and he approached the counter, trying to remember what he came for. "I need coffee, beans, a sack of oats, tobacco, and shells."

The keeper scurried around gathering the items, while Boyd leaned against the counter sucking on a stick candy, picturing green eyes and the prettiest face west of the Mississippi.

After settling up, he carried his supplies down the side street to the livery stable and stacked them with his tack and gear. The blacksmith had finished with an earlier customer and approached his gelding.

"You in a hurry?"

"Nah, I'm going to head over to the saloon for a while."

"If you need a place to stay and a hot meal, I think there's room over at the boarding house. It's right around the corner. My ma runs it, and she could fatten up a wormy runt pup."

"Thanks. I haven't decided yet," Boyd said with a chuckle, heading up the street toward the saloon.

He pushed through the swinging doors and paused to let his eyes adjust to the dim interior. A couple of men sat at a table near the wall, engrossed in a quiet conversation. A lone cowpoke sat folded over his drink at the end of the bar. The barkeep leaned on the bar and flipped the pages of a dime novel, moving his lips as he read.

As Boyd approached the bar, a redhead in a tight blue dress sashayed toward him with a lazy smile on her painted lips.

"Buy a thirsty gal a drink?" She brushed against his arm as she leaned on the bar.

Boyd nodded to the barkeep. "Whiskey, and whatever the lady's drinking." He tossed the first shot of whiskey back and swallowed, allowing the fiery liquid to clear the last few weeks' trail dust from his throat. Holding the empty glass back toward the barkeep, he nodded and smiled as the man refilled it.

He dropped a coin on the bar and carried

the second shot to a nearby table, the redhead following closely. "What's your name, Red?"

"Scarlett," she answered, batting her eyes and leaning forward, allowing the tight dress to showcase her cleavage.

He sipped the whiskey and studied her. Her eyes were bloodshot and tired, nothing like the dancing green eyes he'd tumbled into at the mercantile. Yesterday, he'd have been content to spend his evening and his money with this worn saloon girl, even allowing them both to pretend they were enamored with each other. But today, his mind wouldn't cooperate. He kept seeing the beautiful face of a genuine lady, wondering who she was and where she was. He knew he'd never find anyone like her in a place like this.

Scarlett ran her hands over his arm and rattled on, but he wasn't listening. He gulped the rest of his whiskey and rose to his feet, pulling away from her. "I have to go."

"But wait! We were just getting acquainted."

"No, we weren't." He turned and strode from the bar, escaping into the dusty street.

He ambled back to the livery stable. The blacksmith had finished shoeing Dunny and left him in a small stall nibbling hay. Boyd found the man near the stove and paid him for his work.

"Decide on a room and meal?" the smithy asked.

"Nah, I'm pretty sorry company, even for myself. Don't wanna inflict that on anybody else. Can me and Dunny bed down out here for the night?"

"It's forty cents a day for him, includes a scoop of oats and all the hay he'll eat or mess up. For sixty, you can bed down with him, use the pump and outhouse out back, and I'll bring you a plate of whatever Ma's feeding the sociable guests."

"Sounds like a bargain." Boyd smiled and extended his hand. "Boyd Watts, pleasure to meet you."

"Harvey Mills. Welcome," the smithy grasped his hand and shook. "No smoking in the barn and no guests."

"That won't be a problem," Boyd replied.

Boyd couldn't explain why he felt so out of sorts. Use to being alone on the trail, he was usually happy to join a card game or visit with a bar gal when he hit town. But neither appealed to him today.

A pair of green eyes and a lovely face flashed in his mind. Such a lady would never cast a second glance at a mangy dog like him. She probably pinched her nose at the smell as soon as she'd turned her back to him at the store. Not that he could blame her. He smelled like a polecat.

He went out to the pump, found the chunk of lye soap atop the post, and scrubbed his hands and arms. Then he stripped off his shirt, bent and ducked his head under the water, scrubbing his face, hair, and chest. He soaped the shirt as best he could, wrung it out and hung it over the clothesline.

Back inside, he pulled a dry shirt out of his bedroll and buttoned it on. He needed a shave and a haircut, a full bath, and a clean set of clothes. He wasn't much in the mood, but headed back up to the main street, considering it. It wouldn't matter, anyway. The green-eyed beauty no doubt belonged to someone else, a banker or a business-man. Beautiful ladies didn't fall in love with cow punchers or bounty hunters. And he'd always been too afraid of settling down to even notice he was missing something. Until now. But he could dream.

Boyd noticed people lining the streets watching. A procession of deputies and posse were bringing prisoners toward the jail.

"That's Pa's horse," a child of five or six shouted, dashing past him toward the wagon carrying the bodies.

That child had no business in the street, and certainly didn't need to see the dead. Boyd stepped forward and grabbed the child by the shoulders, looking down into the freckled face of a little girl. She hollered and kicked wildly, but he held firm, trying to calm her.

"Mister, you better let go of my sister!" A boy of maybe ten rushed up, scowling.

The crowd started dispersing as the procession moved on down the street to the jail. No one seemed to notice the cowboy and the two children.

Boyd tried to reason with the boy without letting the girl go. Amid the yelling, he determined the children recognized a horse tied behind the wagon as belonging to their father. Boyd knew the tied horses usually belonged to the dead men. He couldn't let the children see their father piled in the wagon like cordwood.

He kneeled to look the boy in the eyes, keeping a firm hold on the squirming girl. "Son, if that's your Pa's horse, your little sister doesn't need to run up and see what might be in that wagon. Do you understand me?"

74

"Yes, sir," Ben whispered, his eyes swimming.

"What's your name, son?"

"Ben. Benjamin Jeffers."

"Hello, Ben. I'm Boyd Watts. I'm pleased to meet you. Now, I understand you recognize one of those horses. Are you sure?" He kept his voice low and calm, like he was sharing a secret with the kids.

"Yes, sir, Mr. Watts. The blue roan gelding belongs to our Pa. He's got a crescent moon shaped scar on his right front fetlock. Blue does, not Pa," Ben hurried to add.

"Okay. How about you take your sister home? I'll go over to the jail and see what's happening. I'll make sure it's Blue, and let them know who he belongs to. Maybe find out where your pa is. Can you take her home?"

Ben nodded.

They both glanced at his sister. She looked like a barn cat that had been tossed into the water trough. She'd stopped kicking and hollering, but her eyes glared at them both.

"Son, what's your Pa's name?"

Ben squared his shoulders, pulling himself up to his full four-foot, four-inch height. "Rolland Jeffers, Deputy US Marshal."

Boyd's eyes widened. "Take your sister home. I'll find you after I know something."

■ ■ ■ ■

Boyd was standing beside the blue roan, talking with a guard, when the smithy rushed up. Surprised to see the man, he spoke. "Harvey."

Harvey nodded and addressed the guard. "Where's Rolland?"

The guard shook his head. "I dunno. He ain't here."

"Pete, you know dang well that's Rolland's horse. Did they bring him in wounded or dead?"

Boyd watched the exchange in silence. The two men knew each other well, and this didn't involve him.

"Neither, Harvey. Rolland ain't here and no one's seen him."

"Are you sure? Where's the dead they brought in?" Harvey looked around for the wagon.

"Of course I'm sure. I've known Rolland as long as I've known you."

"I've got to see," Harvey said, striding toward a wagon stopped near the rear entrance of the jail.

"You don't believe me?" the guard asked incredulously.

"When my sister asks me if I am positive

he wasn't in the casualties, I need to be able to tell her I made absolutely sure." Harvey turned and rushed into the court house.

"His sister?" Boyd asked.

"Yep. Marshal Jeffers is married to Harvey's sister. They live in the rooming house next to the livery stable. Harvey's ma runs the place."

"So those kids were . . ." Boyd let his words trail off. He was still trying to make sense of the whole thing.

"Yep. They're Harvey's niece and nephew. He's crazy about 'em, too."

"Well, I knew kids didn't have no business seeing a wagonload of dead and dying."

"You're right. And Harvey'll be mighty glad you stepped in and sent them home."

When Harvey returned, he took the gelding's reins. "Thank God, he's not here. One of the prisoners claimed they found the horse wandering near a river over in Indian Territory. They're going to get a scout who knows the area, and he and I will head out to search at first light. Boyd, you headed back to the stable?"

"Yep, I'll walk with you." As they started up the dusty street, Boyd said, "I didn't know they were your kin. I just knew they didn't need to see that wagon up close."

"Let me guess," Harvey said. "Jo-Jo was

77

headed straight for it once she saw her pa's horse."

"Is she part bobcat? It was about all I could do to hold her back without hurting her."

Harvey chuckled. "I believe that."

After putting the roan in a stall, Boyd followed Harvey across a small garden patch and through the back door to a kitchen. A wonderful aroma assaulted his nose and his stomach growled. Then all thought of his appetite vanished.

Turning from the stove was the green-eyed beauty he'd been thinking of all day. He was speechless. The enchanting lady he'd been smitten with was not only married, but she was married to a deputy marshal. The Good Lord must either have a wicked sense of humor or a mean streak.

She was intent on what Harvey was saying and didn't even glance at him.

Boyd studied the floor, wishing he was anywhere but here.

Harvey had just said he was going to search when an older woman interrupted. "Harvey, you're no lawman."

Boyd broke his silence. "She's right. Besides, your family needs you here. I'll go. I'll find Rolland. You have my word."

The women turned to look at him for the

first time. The lovely green-eyes showed no sign of recognition. "Who are you?"

"Boyd Watts, ma'am. I'm a bounty hunter in the Indian territory. I always get my man."

"My husband is no outlaw, Mr. Watts." Her voice was sharp as a blade.

"I understand that, ma'am. But if I can track down rotten scoundrels who don't want to be found, I'm sure I can track down a lawman who does."

The green eyes locked on his, studying him. Finally, she nodded.

His stomach clenched. *What in the world have I done?* "It's settled then. I'll head out at daybreak. Harvey, I'll need you to introduce me to that scout."

As they went out the door, Boyd shook his head. *Dang, I'm a dimwit! What have I gotten myself into now?*

Boyd rode Dunny along the rocky trail, ponying a loaded packhorse. The scout, an Indian named Peck, rode slightly ahead. Peck hadn't said more than a dozen words since they'd mounted up hours earlier. Boyd wasn't sure whether it was because the man's English was limited, he didn't trust his traveling companion, or if he was just a quiet man.

Boyd didn't much care though, since he had a pretty serious conversation going on inside his own head. What exactly did he hope to gain from this venture? There was no bounty to be collected. And he had to admit he didn't really want to reunite the beautiful woman with her husband. But he also couldn't imagine returning to her empty-handed. Or worse, telling her that her husband was dead. Seeing heartbreak or sadness in those gorgeous eyes was more than he could stand. And being the cause of it was unthinkable. No matter which way he wallowed the facts, this mission was doomed. If he was smart, he'd ride away and never return to this particular little border town. But he'd never been called smart.

Day three on the trail, and Peck had spoken only when it was necessary. They'd only traveled an hour or so from the grove where they'd made camp. Suddenly, something smacked into Boyd's chest hard enough to knock him backwards.

Before he had time to realize it, he was tumbling from the saddle as Dunny leaped forward. He landed hard on his back in the dirt. The horses' hooves stirred clouds of dust as they disappeared up the trail.

With the breath knocked out of him, he could not move or think for a minute. Finally, he dragged himself a few feet to the nearest tree and struggled to prop himself against the trunk. Exhausted, he closed his eyes. He needed to rest a minute, then he'd try to figure out what was happening.

"Boyd," a soft voice called.

He forced first one eye, then the other, to open. An angelic face with dancing green eyes smiled at him. The face he'd been seeing in his mind for days, complete with auburn hair in a loose braid, falling over one shoulder of her bluebonnet-colored dress. Behind her, a wooden porch held two rocking chairs. He tried to swallow a lump in his throat.

"Supper's almost ready. Better hurry and get washed up."

He reached his hand toward her.

She smiled and reached toward him, letting her fingertips brush across his wrist and hand. "Come on."

Boyd's hand flopped into the dirt. Pain blinded him. He gasped for air. He blinked his eyes and looked down at the dark blood that soaked his shirt and spread across his lap. Up the trail, he saw an unmoving mound of cloth that was likely Peck. He tried to draw in a breath and felt more than heard the horrible raspy gurgle.

Exhaustion swept his mind, and his eyes dropped closed.

"Don't take too long," the gentle voice said.

Boyd's eyes opened in time to catch a flash of bluebonnet-colored skirt disappear into the door of a cabin. He closed his eyes and followed her, a smile curving his lips. Maybe God didn't have such a mean streak after all.

MERCY AIN'T NO PREACHER

BY GARY RODGERS

The sound of horses racing into town disrupted Sunday morning service at Canaan Union Church. Will Hayes motioned for Pastor Wade to stay in the pulpit as he rose to check on the noise outside. As he stepped outside, he drew his Colt pistol, then the shooting began.

Pastor Chase Wade raced to bar the door shut, but it slammed open as he slid to a stop. Three gunmen blocked the doorway with guns drawn. Chase could see Will Hayes lying face first on the church steps. A fourth man approached, and the three parted to allow him entry to the church.

"What do you want here?" Chase growled.

"Well now, Preacher, I would like to speak to your flock this fine morning. I already found one stray sheep I came looking for, and I need your flocks' help to locate two more. You just mind your tone, and we'll be on our way soon enough."

Chase followed the unwelcome guest to the pulpit. If this man needed someone to make an example of, he wanted it to be himself, not one of his parishioners. If the man underestimated Chase, he would make him pay for his poor judgement.

Pulling an Army Colt from its holster, the new guest spoke. "Pastor, why don't you have a seat in the front row? You seem mighty sure of yourself. I really don't want to start my Sunday killing a man of the cloth," he smiled. "That's more of a Friday night kind of thing."

The men in the doorway laughed at the comment. Chase didn't find it funny.

"Will Hayes was a good man," Chase barked. "He didn't deserve to be gunned down like a dog in the street."

With a stare at Chase, the man spoke. "Corporal Hayes, now recently departed, was a traitor to the Confederacy. I came here to find him and two more men. Sargeant Matthew Walker, and Captain Miles Jackson. I am colonel Grant Wilkerson. And I know they are from here, because they held me and my men prisoner in St. Louis. They talked about their fine town of Canaan, Arkansas all the time. And I've been told Captain Miles is now the sheriff. So, if you fine folks will tell me where these

84

men are, I can conclude my business and we will be on our way."

The small church crowd sat silent.

"Now!" The Colonel shouted as he fired his Colt into the ceiling.

"You have poor timing, Colonel," Chase spoke as he took a seat in the front row. "Besides the fact the war ended over a year ago, Matt and Miles left last week for Fort Smith."

"They'll be back by the day after tomorrow. My pa said so," a youngster spoke up.

Chase grimaced at the smile on the Colonel's face. "It's nice to know we still have supporters in this town. I fear your preacher might not feel the same way, young man. I reckon you stayed home for the war, Preacher. Am I right?"

"No." Chase looked around at his church. "I fought for the Confederacy at Arkansas Post, Vicksburg, and Pea Ridge. Along with plenty of skirmishes in between. When the war ended, so did my fight. I came back here to take the church my daddy started. It's time you realize the war is over and stop killing innocent men."

"Innocent! Ha! No southerner who fought for the north in the war is innocent. I will hang both of them for treason when they return. In the meantime, Preacher, you can have some of these ladies cook up a decent meal for me and my men. Or the hanging might start with you."

Chase weighed the situation and knew these men would kill or injure too many of his friends if he or anyone else resisted. Rising from his seat, he turned and studied his small congregation. Canaan only had forty or fifty people living in or close by, and half of them were here. He couldn't expect any help from the ones not in church. He needed a look outside to see if more than the four men in the church accompanied Wilkerson.

"Mister, I believe I can have a few of these women fix up a meal. But would you allow some of these men to move Will's body out of the street before the women go out there? They don't need to see him."

"Corporal Anderson, tell the men outside to keep watch on whoever moves that traitor out of the street." A man turned and walked outside. "Preacher, you can have two men move his body, then come back in here and have a seat. But first, I want you to go around and gather up all the pistol belts off everyone. We don't want anybody getting heroic in here, now do we?"

Chase chose two younger men to move the body and collected their gun belts. As they walked outside, he looked out the door long enough to learn three more men waited outside. Seven in total. He continued collecting belts and carried them to the pulpit.

"Preacher, I saw you taking stock of the situation. Maybe you were a fine soldier during the war. But I don't recommend you get any ideas. My men are good too. A town like this needs its preacher. I'd hate to kill you for being too brave."

"It's a soulless man willing to kill a preacher," an older lady spoke out.

The Colonel smiled at the lady before answering. "Ma'am, my daddy was a preacher. He used to whip me every day of the week. Beat my mama too. When I came in from chopping wood at fourteen and found mama near dead, I stopped him. Put an axe in the back of his head and cussed him till he quit kicking. So, I know what kind of man a preacher can be. Mercy ain't no preacher."

The sound of running steps drew the Colonel's attention to the doorway.

Corporal Anderson stepped in the door. "Rider coming, Colonel. Fast."

The Colonel forced Chase to the doorway and watched as a rider raced into town to the boarding house. It was a woman. She slid off her horse and hurried inside.

"That's Mattie Hill. She has a place a mile out of town. Doc Baker lives at the boarding house. I'm guessing she came for the doctor," Chase said, not mentioning her young son not being with her.

The Colonel turned on Chase to see his eyes, then smiled.

"I see a spark in them eyes, Preacher. Maybe you should take two of these ladies over there to fix some food for me and the boys. Then bring that lady back here with you. Just remember, this fine flock is counting on you to not do anything stupid," he snarled.

"I won't do anything to put these people at risk. But if she doesn't want to come back here, I won't be able to make her."

"Convince her it's in her best interest. And yours. Now get to it. Anderson, you go with him."

Chase motioned for two of the older ladies to join him and walked out of the church feeling guilty. If anything happened to the people inside, he wouldn't forgive himself. But he felt certain Mattie hadn't come to the boarding house without her son unless something was wrong. He needed to know what it might be,

"Ladies, start cooking lunch for everybody." Chase motioned as they entered the lobby of the boarding house. "I'll find Mattie and head back to the church."

"Hold up there," Anderson protested. "Let me have a look in that kitchen before you ladies go in there."

The ladies stepped back toward Chase as Anderson pushed the door open to stick his head inside. Chase turned to see if he could see anything of Mattie in the other rooms.

Clang! Followed by a loud thud made Chase turn back to the kitchen. Anderson lay sprawled out on the floor.

"Mattie?" Chase whispers.

"No. But she helped set it up." Sheriff Jackson said as he stepped from behind the door.

"Sheriff? You weren't supposed to be back for two more days. But I'm glad to see you," Chase said.

"It's Deputy Marshal now, Preacher. It's why I went to Fort Smith. There are a dozen men waiting outside town for me. They showed me a telegraph in Fort Smith three days ago about Colonel Wilkerson and his men being in the area. I figured he planned to find me, and Will and Matt. I wish I'd gotten here before he found Will. Doc Baker saw what was happening over at the church and rode out to Mattie's. We stopped there on our way into town. Is everyone okay at the church?"

"For now." Chase said. "But the Colonel is smart. He'll know something is up if I don't get back there. You ladies get in there and get the fire going, so he knows someone's in the kitchen. Where's Mattie?"

"She's out back with my horse. I wanted her to hightail it out-of-town if anything went wrong. Wilkerson and his men killed a dozen men in Missouri before they rode here. This needs to be their last stop."

"Good, good. I need to get some things from upstairs. I'll be back down in a minute." Chase ran up the stairs.

In his room, Chase threw the frock coat on the bed and stared into the mirror. The man looking back at him differed from the one he faced early that morning. The collar around his neck felt like it didn't belong. With a jerk, he ripped it off and flung it on the dresser, then reached for the gunbelt hanging on the wall. It suited the man in the mirror better than the collar.

At the foot of the stairs, Chase turned when the back door opened, his gun leaping into his hand. It was Mattie. He holstered the Colt as he walked to her.

"Mattie, you need to go home. It's going to be too dangerous for you in town."

"Now there's the Chase Wade I used to

know," Mattie answered. "Always telling me what to do, but too shy to come visit me at home. I'll go home when my friends are safe. After I know you haven't gone and got yourself killed."

"You two catch up later," Marshal Miles said. "The Colonel won't wait all day."

"Sheriff. Uh, Marshal. What do I call you, Miles?"

"Marshal is fine, Chase."

"I need to get to the back of the church. Daddy built a trapdoor in the floor by the pulpit. If I can get inside without them seeing me, maybe we can keep anyone inside from getting hurt."

"Mattie, we might need your help again," the marshal said.

"I'll do it." She answered.

"Chase, you make your way around behind the church. I already have three men watching the livery stable, waiting for my signal. When I see you at the church, I'll have Mattie get the Colonel's attention."

"Don't put her in danger, Marshal. We can find another way."

"Chase, we're all in danger as long as that man lives. Now here." The marshal reached into his vest pocket and pulled out a silver star. "I appoint you Sheriff of Canaan. Consider it a last act of goodwill to the people of Canaan."

Chase considered arguing but knew now wasn't the time. A look at the star, and he placed it in his pocket and rushed out the back door. He'd settle this with the marshal later.

"Preacher, what's taking so long in there? Do I need to drag one of these fine folks out in the street and shoot them for you to come back?" Colonel Wilkerson shouted from the steps of the church.

From behind the boarding house, Chase answered. "Like I said, Colonel, she's a stubborn woman." Then he ran behind the general store, hoping to not answer again. The way Canaan laid out, he could get to the church from there without being seen.

Once behind the church, he waved to the marshal. He didn't expect what came next.

"Go to hell, Preacher. I ain't going over there with you now or ever," Mattie screamed as she stormed out of the boarding house and climbed onto the horse tied in front.

Colonel Wilkerson stormed off the church steps into the street, screaming. "Hold it right there, Miss. You ain't going nowhere."

Chase had already made it to the trapdoor and inside the church when the Colonel began shouting. Neither of the men inside heard him until the door fell shut. Before they could turn, Chase shot both men and ran to the front door. A volley of shots rang out from behind the livery stable as he reached the door.

Colonel Wilkerson turned at the sound of gunshots inside the church in time to see two of his men fall outside. With the realization of being outflanked, he ran for the boarding house, looking back and firing as he ran. Chase ran out of the church in time for what happened in the street to strike fear in his heart.

Colonel Wilkerson turned back toward the boarding house at the sound of horse hooves charging at him. Mattie had turned her horse toward him and urged it to lunge in his direction. The Colonel raised his pistol and fired twice. The marshal fired a rifle from the steps of the boarding house and Chase emptied his Colt, knocking the Colonel to the ground in a hail of bullets.

Chase's heart sank when he saw Mattie's head jerk back and her body slide from the saddle onto the hard packed earth, tumbling, then laying still.

He ran to her side, praying she wasn't dead. A deep gash cut across her temple and above her ear. Blood trickled down the side of her face as he cradled her in his arms and stroked her hair.

"Mattie. Wake up. You hear me? Don't you die on me now."

A scowl formed on her forehead as she opened her eyes. "Chase? Why am I laying in the street? Ouch! My head feels like I've been kicked by a mule. What happened?"

"You got shot, Mattie. What were you thinking? Charging him like that. Let me see how bad it is."

"She okay?" the marshal asked.

"Looks like it creased her good. With her hard head, she should be fine. But we need the doctor to look at her."

"Matt, take one of my deputies with you and bring Doc Baker and Mattie's son into town."

"I should have killed you first, Preacher." Colonel Wilkerson said as he made it to his knees. Blood covered his chest and ran out the side of his mouth. "But now will have to do."

His right arm hung limp at his side as he raised a pistol in his left. Chase had forgotten to load his pistol after emptying it into him. Marshal Miles reached for his pistol, only to find it gone. Chase had it, firing two shots into Wilkerson. One knocked the pistol from Wilkerson's hand as the other tore through the man's shoulder and knocked him backwards.

Chase rose from his knees and loaded his pistol as he walked toward the Colonel. Everyone from inside the church had made it outside now, and all of Colonel Wilkerson's men were dead. While Chase felt hatred for the man, an odd sensation of admiration came over him as the Colonel forced himself back to his knees.

"Let him be, Chase." Marshal Miles growled. "If Doc Baker can get him patched up, I'll take him back to Fort Smith to hang."

Several church goers made a line between Chase and Marshal Miles. He knew what was about to happen, and he knew his job was to stop it. Or was it?

"You hear that, Preacher. He wants to hang me. How do you feel about that?" Colonel Wilkerson croaked through the blood choking his throat.

"This country is changing, Colonel. The war is over. Men like you can't go around killing honest folks."

"Preacher, men like me will always keep men like you honest."

"You said it earlier, Colonel. Mercy ain't no preacher. Well, neither am I." Chase fired a last shot between the eyes of his tormentor.

Turning back, he could see Mattie on her feet with the help of some other women. He looked at her and knew she understood the necessity of his actions. But would she still respect him?

Chase walked to her and placed his arm around her waist, then began leading her to the boarding house. He felt her lean against him as if she belonged there.

"I never came out to see you after Buell died in the flood. I should have Mattie, and I'm sorry I didn't. But I would very much like to come out now, if it's okay with you?"

"Chase, I told you before you went off to the war, I could be a lot of things, but not a preacher's wife. You had no reason to think that had changed."

"I could use that as an excuse, but I won't. And now, I don't have to. How would you feel about the new sheriff of Canaan courting you?"

"Depends. Is he gonna hunt outlaws during the week and preach on Sunday? Or will he have time to help raise a youngster and care for a little farm?"

"Canaan can find another preacher, Mattie. I already know there's only one you."

"You gonna pin that star on, Chase?" Marshal Jackson interrupted. "Or do I need to take you in for killing an unarmed man?"

Chase pulled the star from his pocket and pinned it to his chest. An approving glance from Mattie told him he made the right choice.

THE LAST RIDE

BY RHONDA ROBERTS

"Gimme that *mochila,* boy, or I'll kill ya!"

Johnny Adams flattened himself against his little mustang pony as they galloped up the trail. Sweat waterfalled into his eyes, and blood poured from his right cheek, the mark of Bull Campbell's first attempt to shoot him. Johnny's Pony Express mail pouch, or mochila, rode snug on his saddle, and Johnny wasn't about to give it up before he reached Carson City.

"I'm gonna get you, boy, and that mochila will be mine anyway. This is your last ride!"

Bull, with his fresh mount, was forcing them off the trail. Johnny urged his tired pony up the ridge, through scrub brush and rocky terrain, struggling to keep Bull from getting a clear shot at him. Any other day, he would have enjoyed the fiery sunset. Today, he just hoped the sun would hurry up and set so he could hide in the dark.

Trying to hide the desperation in his

voice, Johnny called over his shoulder to his pursuer. "Let me go on through, Bull. Ain't no money, just letters in this bag."

"That's what ole Jack Borden said, too, but I found ten dollars in them letters he carried."

Fear clutched at Johnny's heart. Then something else bubbled up from deep inside him.

Rage.

"You broke your company oath, Bull! You swore before God not to quarrel or fight with any other Pony Express employee. You, you killed Jackie for ten dollars! And made it look like Indians did it!"

"I don't work for the Express no more, boy. Masterson fired me 'cause I wouldn't ride through the middle of a Injun war. Little ole Jack shoulda gave me the bag. He's not the first I've scalped, and won't be the last — but you'll be next!"

Limbs and briars tore at Johnny's face and clothes as they crashed through the trees.

"If you're not riding for the Express, what're you doing out here?"

"Robbin' you, that's what. Easier than robbin' a train, since it's only me an' you. An' even if there ain't no money in that pouch, I reckon there'll be papers. Somebody'll pay dearly to get 'em back. Or somebody'd love to get ahold of 'em an' keep 'em from getting where they're goin'."

Johnny's mustang stumbled, nearly falling to its knees. The relief station he had reached earlier that day had been abandoned, and with no fresh mount, he'd had no choice but to keep going on his exhausted one. That was the way it was for a Pony Express rider. You did what you had to do until you were done.

What Bull didn't know was that this really was Johnny's last ride. The new transcontinental telegraph would begin operating in a week, and the Pony Express just couldn't compete. Johnny's boss had sent him on one last run. Documents from Washington that needed to be hand delivered to officials in Carson City, letters to family members, it didn't matter what the courier pouch held. It was his job, and he was going to complete it.

And Johnny had another reason to make it to Carson City.

Emma.

The first time he met her, she was outside the General Store, waiting on her father. As soon as he saw her, Johnny was totally smitten. He couldn't take his eyes off her, just sat on his pony and stared. He memorized every facet of her face in that first glance.

She watched him, and the smile that played on her lips reached all the way up to crinkle the corners of her brown eyes.

"Are you going to stay on your horse all afternoon?"

Her voice was soft, and it seemed to Johnny like she had sung those words. He would have stayed on his mount for the rest of his life, just to hear her voice.

A raucous shout from across the street brought him back to his senses. He swung his leg over the saddle to jump down, only to catch his heel on the stirrup. If he hadn't grabbed the reins to steady himself, he would have landed face down in the dirt.

He braced himself for her laughter, but it never came. She just kept the same pleasant expression she had before, as if his dismount had been perfectly normal. At that moment, Johnny realized that this lady was different from anyone he had ever met. He saw in her sparkling eyes truer kindness than he had ever known. He had just met her, and he didn't even know her name, but his heart was hers.

After that, Johnny took every trip to Carson City he could get. Time went by, and to his everlasting amazement, he discovered Emma felt the same way about him. And she was waiting for him. That was powerful motivation to finish his ride alive.

Reaching the cover of a rock outcropping, Johnny jumped to the ground, grabbed the mochila off the saddle and whacked the mustang on the rump. It stumbled off down the trail, giving Johnny a split second to scramble behind the boulders before Bull caught up to him.

The long shadows cast on the rocks by the setting sun gave Johnny a chance. Bull was so certain he would win that he made no attempt to be quiet as he charged up the trail. When he realized Johnny no longer rode the mustang, Bull roared. A single shot and a scream from his pony meant the end of Johnny's mount. Johnny had no time to grieve for that good horse as he crept up the ridge, his soft leather boots making very little noise on the rocky ground.

"You can't hide from me, boy! I'm gonna gut you!"

In the fading light, Johnny saw Bull dismount. As he clambered over the loose soil, a shower of stones skittered down the slope.

"You've got nowhere to go now, boy." Bull wheezed and grunted with the effort to keep his footing. "There ain't no point to this nohow. Your job . . . is over. No, no more Pony Express. No more . . . need for you. There's nothin' in that bag worth dying for, right? C'mon out now. Gimme that pouch. I'll let you walk away."

Johnny clamped his mouth shut. His heart pounded as he heard Bull working his way toward his hiding place. There was no way Bull would ever let him live.

"You won't . . . even have a job after tomorrow, boy. Then what, what're you gonna do? Herd cows? Grow crops? Think you can tolerate sittin' in one place? Farmin' after all the ridin' you've done? All the country you seen?"

Bull cursed and Johnny heard him slip in the dark, rocks tumbling as he scrambled to stop sliding backwards.

Johnny wedged himself between two huge boulders. If he tried to creep away in the dark, he was just as likely to fall off the side of the ridge, or give away his position. He clutched the mochila in his arms. A tiny voice in his head asked him if that pouch was really worth dying for. A stronger voice told him he was not going to die. He had too much to live for.

"You might take up soldiering, boy. Would, would you like killin' folks for a livin'? It's not so bad once you get used to it. I got used to it a long time ago."

Bull's voice was just below him. In a matter of moments, Johnny would be found.

103

He clutched the pouch in one arm and felt along the ground until his hand closed around a rock. It was the only weapon he had.

"Soldierin'll get ya killed, though. But you gotta have a job . . . Can't get a woman without any money, can ya?"

Bull was right beside him now, still scanning for any movement. The moon was beginning to rise. Soon, the shadows hiding Johnny would be lost to its eerie glow.

"I heard you have a sweet little thing in Carson City."

A deadly calm settled over Johnny.

"I got me some money. Maybe I'll pay her a visit. Show 'er how a real man —"

Johnny leaped out, slinging the rock at Bull's head. Too slow to react, Bull took the full blow, and as he staggered, the two collided, tumbling toward the edge of the embankment. Gaining his feet first, Johnny kicked the pistol from Bull's grip and it clattered down the rocks. There'd be no way either of them could find it in the dark.

Bull struggled to his feet, wiping the blood from his face. He yelled, "I'll tear you apart, boy! You'll beg to die before I get through with you. I'll cut you to pieces!"

Johnny grabbed a fistful of Bull's shirt. "I may not have a job, but I do have a future!

I won't allow the likes of you to take that from me."

With a roar, Bull shoved him. As Johnny fell back against the boulders, he heard the roar become a cry of shock as Bull reeled backwards. An avalanche of rocks followed him over the edge and down into the valley below.

For a short while Johnny could only lay against the boulder, catching his breath as he gazed into the night sky. He stood; the familiar weight of the mochila still clutched in his hand. He looked toward the edge of the cliff, at the last of the dust drifting downward in the moonlight. "I guess this was your last ride, too."

Gingerly making his way down the embankment, he found Bull's horse beside the trail. He draped the mochila over the saddle and patted the horse on the neck. "Let's go home," he told it. Mounting the horse, he set off once again for Carson City; after all, you did what you had to do until you were done. And after the job was done, he knew Emma would be waiting for him.

PULLING TEETH

BY DON MONEY

If the man in the chair didn't kill him, this might turn out to be a good day for Easton Hughes. After two months in Croton Springs, his jack of all trades business was finally picking up. The town was a dusty little watering hole in Cochise County along the Tucson Cutoff. Easton, slight of build and with a shock of red hair, set up shop to provide everything from a haircut, to repairing boots, to dental work.

Easton's ability to provide a variety of services landed many people in the chair in his store. Mostly ordinary folks, but Easton knew some would provide him with a great story to spin at the saloon later that night. This was one of those people, that is, if the man in the chair wanting a tooth pulled didn't kill him first. The man had walked in off of the street and proceeded to sit down in the chair uttering a few simple words. His customer was known to be fast and handy with either the Colt revolver or the Bowie knife he carried.

"The back one, top right side, you say?" Easton said as he draped a cape over the front of the man to protect the blue shirt, should any blood try to drip on it. His nerves were on edge.

"That is correct," came the reply, clipped at having to confirm a pretty simple instruction.

Easton pulled some pliers off the counter-top and walked back over to the customer who sat in his work chair, facing the open door to the street just beyond.

The customer eyed the tool with some concern. "I know you aren't about to stick those in my mouth as dirty as they are. Oral health is just as important as keeping oneself from getting poked open by a knife."

"No, sir," Easton stammered, "I was just about to clean them off."

"Sterilize them, you mean."

"Yeah, yeah, yeah," Easton said. He didn't quite know what that word meant, but he got the idea he needed to figure it out if he wanted to keep an existence on the right side of the grass.

"I graduated from the Pennsylvania College of Dental Surgery. What about you?" the customer asked Easton.

Easton became queasy. Would this be the thing to set his customer off? He had heard stories about the man's patience, or lack thereof. "No training. Just something I've picked up along the way, same as giving a haircut or replacing the sole of a man's boot."

"Except neither of those things are going to cause a man pain, least they shouldn't be. How many teeth have you pulled?"

"A couple of dozen," Easton said.

"Have you ever done any other dental work?"

Easton noticed the man's arm moving under the cape draped over his front. "No sir. I leave all that other stuff to the professionals."

"Good answer," the customer replied. "Proceed with the cleaning."

Walking over to the washbasin, Easton splashed the pliers in the water, hoping this would pass muster for the customer. He turned with the freshly cleaned tool and walked back over to his customer.

"So that's your way to sterilize, that's all you do?" the man said, a small smile creeping up on his face.

"Generally, but I'd be happy to do anything else you would like."

"No sir. That will do for me," the man

replied. "Just sit over there with them by your counter and let them dry real well."

"Dry? For how long?"

"Shouldn't be much longer now. Just stay over there with them, away from the door and out of the way."

Easton heard the distinctive click of the hammer of a revolver clicking back under the customer's cape. Maybe he should clean the pliers a little better, Easton thought.

The sounds on the street outside seemed to have gone silent. "Got mighty quiet out there," Easton said. He felt nervous and uneasy and wanted to fill the void with words. "Must be a fight coming. Probably some grudge from the trail spilled into town."

The customer eyed Easton. "I didn't catch your name when I came in here, shopkeeper."

"Easton, sir. Easton Hughes." Easton stood up to proffer his hand with the introduction.

"Have a seat," the customer said. "The show is about to start."

As the words left the man's mouth, a large shape filled the doorway of the shop. "Heard you were in town looking for my brothers and me," growled the voice from the door.

"There you are, Billy Slash. Where's Zeke

and Patton?" came the smooth reply from the chair.

"They are right outside," Billy said. "They wouldn't miss seeing their oldest brother kill Doc Holliday."

Doc smiled. "Now, let's not get ahead of ourselves, Billy. I am the aggrieved party here. You boys are the ones who stole the money from my room in Bisbee as I was off having a drink and playing a little faro. As to be expected, though. Word always was the Slash brothers were cowards."

With that provocation, Billy went for the pistol on his side, but barely touched the handle when a shot blasted from underneath the cape over Doc Holliday. The shot caught the man in the chest and he fell back into the street.

Instantly, with cat reflexes, Doc sprang from the chair and moved toward the door as Zeke Slash entered with a shotgun in hand. Doc was faster once again and two trigger pulls sent Zeke crumpling to the floor.

Doc went low through the door as a shot splintered the frame. Patton Slash fired another round that clipped Holliday's arm, causing him to drop his revolver.

The Bowie knife slid clean from its sheath as Doc bulldogged ahead, closing the gap, and buried the blade in Patton's stomach.

"Not so tough when facing the iron or blade, huh, boys?" Doc remarked to the three dead bodies.

Easton Hughes sat in shock in the shop when Doc Holliday walked back in and flipped a coin in his direction. "Here is for your time and the seat," Doc said.

Stunned, Easton replied, "What about your tooth, Mr. Holliday?"

"Didn't really need pulling," Doc said. "I just need to be in a way where those brothers would lower their guard and think they had the drop on me."

Easton pocketed the coin, knowing he would indeed have the best story in the saloon tonight.

Doc called back over his shoulder as he walked out, "Besides, your sterilization technique leaves a little to be desired."

DISCOVERY NEAR IDAHO SPRINGS

BY ELLEN E. WITHERS

Jud Sterling scanned the horizon. His breath made white, cloudlike puffs in the crisp air. Little time remained, a few days at most, before the easy autumn turned into a fierce winter. He had to recover six strays from his herd. Fast.

The sun had waltzed from the flat plains to the rock face and now its orange tendrils nudged the summit of the Rocky Mountains. The jagged edge of the sheer cliffs beside him was a towering reminder of supremacy.

Shifting in his saddle, he spotted a black speck halfway up the nearby hillside. What was that? Darker than one of his strays, yet too small to be a man. Or was it?

He eased his mount toward the sighting. Buck, his herd dog, followed behind.

When Jud reached the black lump, he slid from his saddle. His worn boots scattered loose rocks as he moved to inspect his find.

A small, pale hand extended from a tattered sleeve. A woman. Was she alive? He felt for a pulse. Finding a spark of life, he heaved a sigh of relief.

Then he took a closer look at the face.

This wasn't a woman. The tangled mess of golden hair could belong to a boy or a girl, yet the bones of the face showed the promise of a strong jaw. Bruises purpled his jawline, the left eye, and the nose. Worn britches and boots jutted below a thin coat. A boy? Had to be a boy. Eight or nine? He wasn't sure. He'd never spent much time around children.

He'd either been beaten or had fallen. After a quick glance, he deduced the boy hadn't fallen from the rocks above. Such an impact would have left more than bruises. Did he collapse from exhaustion? Where had he come from and where was he going?

A word of warning shooed Buck's curious nose away from the lad. Jud gathered the bedroll from his saddle and carefully wrapped the boy's torn body. He heaved him on his shoulder and mounted his horse. The sure-footed horse carefully picked her way down the rocky ridge.

Upset by the boy's unconsciousness, Jud wondered what to do. Rest and warmth would help, but this little guy couldn't stay more than a night. Once the snow arrived, he'd be stuck with him for months.

They headed east to his small cabin. Perhaps warmth and a bit of bread would heal the child.

By nightfall, when his patient began to stir in the bed, Jud felt a sense of relief. Jud marked his place in his book with a worn strip of leather. Must have been hours without movement from the lad.

He pulled a chair to the side of the bed. The lad's brown eyes soon opened and focused on his face. In an instant, fear painted the boy's bruised face.

"Partner, there's no need for you to be scared of me," he said in a deep baritone, trying to ease the scowl that was his natural facial configuration.

The child stared at him, his mouth a tight, colorless line.

"What's your name, son?"

The boy licked dry lips and said, "William."

Jud rose and found a tin cup. After a quick dip in the water bucket, William gulped the contents and handed it back with wobbly effort.

"Are you from around here, son?"

"No, sir."

"Why were you in the mountains?"

William's eyes darted like a cornered cub. After a pause, he came to a decision. "I was running away."

"From what?"

"My Pappy, sir."

He studied the boy's sunken eyes and bruised face. Now he knew a fall hadn't caused the damage to the boy's face. Only a scoundrel could beat a child. What had been his crime?

"Winter's only days away. If I hadn't found you, you'd have frozen to death."

William blinked his surprise at this revelation, and then hung his head. "I didn't know."

"There's some rabbit stew warming near the fire. Reckon you'd take a bite or two?"

William nodded his agreement.

After filling a bowl, Jud watched him gobble the stew. "Bet your ma's worried about you."

After a pause, the boy said in a shaky voice, "She's dead." He scraped the bottom of the bowl with his spoon.

Jud took the empty bowl, re-filled it, then watched in silence as William attacked it with renewed enthusiasm.

"Are you from Idaho Springs?"

William nodded. "Pappy heard there's money to be made mining gold. We come from St. Joe. Worked our way west."

Gold fever lured many people here. Some good, some bad.

Jud looked up a moment later and William was asleep, so the cowboy returned to the fire and his book. Poor little lad. He couldn't imagine his past life.

The following morning, Jud woke with a start from his rocking chair, the victim of his own loud snores. Stiffness permeated his back and neck. Damn kid. He'd be damned if he was going to sleep in a chair another night.

Jud walked over to the boy and felt a tiny twinge of guilt over his anger. The lad's curly hair stuck out at all angles; black eyelashes brushed against bruised skin.

He turned to start a fire. Breakfast would help the youngster.

At Jud's first call, William scrambled out of bed and made quick work of his porridge.

"Mister?"

"Yes?"

"What's your name?"

"Jud."

"I ain't never called no adult by their first name."

"You can start now," Jud replied. "Are you feeling better?"

William nodded.

116

"Think you can ride with me?"

"Yes, sir. Where to, Mister Jud?"

"Back to Idaho Springs and your Pappy."

Tears welled in the boy's eyes.

Jud studied the boy and his bruises. A sharp pain stabbed his heart. "Won't your Pappy be worried about you?"

Before he could blink, the boy bolted out the door. Jud ran after him, fury rising with every step.

In the yard, Buck joined in the chase, barking at the fleeing boy like he was a stray from the herd. William was ten feet from the barn when Jud caught his collar and twisted the material until William yelped. Tight-lipped, Jud led him back into the cabin and plopped him in a chair.

"Like it or not, William, you're going back to your father."

The lad sobbed.

Jud watched him for a minute, remaining silent. He felt like he'd kicked Buck. Damn kid. *Why'd I have to find him?*

"William, you're a child. You belong with your father."

William covered his face with his palms. The silence broken only by sniffling.

"What's his name?"

William wiped his nose on his sleeve and sat mute.

Jud moved beside him and drew the child into his lap.

William wiggled for a moment, then settled against his chest.

"What made your father angry?"

The boy shrugged his shoulders. "Pappy's mad most of the time. I do what he says. I get a whippin' if'n I don't."

"You do your chores?"

"I ain't got no chores. I work with Pappy."

"In the mines?"

"Yes, Mister Jud. Before we come here, we plowed fields or chopped weeds. Whatever work we could get."

Jud looked down at the mop of blonde curls. "You help your father?"

"I do."

Working mines as a child, poor little lad. To a man who loved wide-open spaces, working in darkness beneath the surface of the ground seemed sheer torture.

"What do you do there?"

"I keep the candles lit, shovel a bit, and run buckets to the rail car. I cain't tote a full bucket, but I manage a nearly full one."

"How long have you been mining?"

William paused before he answered. "I reckon about —"

Buck began to bark, followed by the sound of a rider.

William stiffened in his arms.

Jud put the lad back into the chair and then stepped outside.

The rider appeared uncomfortable on the old horse he rode. The animal looked familiar and when they traveled closer, he recognized the worn saddle and bridle, too. Hired from the livery in Idaho Springs. Looks as if William's Pappy saved him the trouble of going into town.

Jud called out to the rider. "Morning."

"Morning," the rider replied, bringing his horse to a stumbling halt. "Name's O'Shey. I'm looking for a runaway. Lad's seven years old. Blonde, curly hair. 'Bout as high as your waist."

Jud waited for the rider to step down, but he remained on his elderly horse.

"I'm Jud Sterling. Care to come inside?"

O'Shey's eyes darted to his. "Do you have a bit of deliverance for a man cold and thirsty?"

Jud nodded. "I've got just the thing for warming up a cold morning."

Jud led O'Shey inside and scanned the room for William. No sign of him anywhere, then a brief smile creased his face when he spotted his lumpy bed.

Jud pulled the cork off his whiskey jug and poured a good measure into a cup. He handed it to his guest and invited him to sit.

In a gulp, the man emptied the cup and banged it upon the table.

Jud filled O'Shey's cup again and watched him pour the fiery liquid down his throat for a second time.

"So you're looking for a boy?"

The man eyed his empty tin cup, then glanced up at him. "Yep."

"How long's he been missing?"

O'Shey's eyes returned to the cup. "Nearly a week."

"A week?" Good Lord. No wonder the boy was hungry.

"I kept thinking he'd come back, the little shit, but then I figured he was hurt. His dead mother would haunt me if I didn't try to find him."

Jud studied the detachment in the man across from him. He didn't seem to care about his son.

"Why'd the boy run away?"

"I took a switch to him. Had to show him to keep his mouth shut."

More than a switch damaged that boy. "What'd he do?"

"Went beggin' for food one night and got me in trouble with the law. I was gonna bring him some grub after relaxin' at Maggie's Place." O'Shey winked at Jud. "You know Maggie's Place, don't you?"

Jud nodded. Every man worth his salt in the territory, including himself, had frequented Maggie and her girls at one time or another.

"When I tried to find him later, he was gone. The next morning, a deputy kicked me awake. The woman that fed him said I was mistreating him. By damn, I whipped him good once I caught up with him. The next morning he was gone."

It had been nearly a week and the "whipping" was still visible on the boy's face. Jud controlled his rage and uncorked the whisky jug, plying the man with another dose.

O'Shey emptied his cup and smacked his lips.

Jud heard the sound of a muffled cough from the boy hiding under the sheets a few feet away. He immediately began coughing. Pulling out his handkerchief, he blew his nose like a bugle. After a moment, he paused. The only sound in the room was the crackle of the fire. He breathed a sigh of relief and returned the handkerchief to his pocket.

A glance at O'Shey found him fingering his empty cup.

"When did his mother die?" Jud asked.

"Over a year now. I'm still angry she left me alone with the brat. Never knew his father, but she was always comparing me to him. I's the sinner, he's the saint."

Jud leaned across the table toward the man. "So the boy isn't yours?"

"You mean my blood? Hell, no. I wasn't even married to his mother. She was penniless after that saint of a husband died. 'Twas a wee bit of kindness that I took in her and the lad."

Jud grunted. He listened to the man yammer a while longer, then stopped him once he'd made up his mind.

"I know you're here to find a boy." Jud drew a deep breath. "But I can't help you."

O'Shey's response to the declaration was to push the empty tin toward Jud. "Would you be sparing a thirsty man one more drink for the road?"

Jud grimaced but filled the tin.

O'Shey threw back the contents and stood to leave. "I'm obliged for the whiskey and warm fire."

Jud nodded and walked the man to the corral.

Back on his hired horse, O'Shey tipped his hat. Then he drew his thin coat together in an effort to block the cold wind and awkwardly kicked the horse westward.

Buck, as with any visitor, walked with O'Shey until satisfied he wasn't coming back.

Jud watched the man and his horse disappear over the horizon.

"The sky will start spitting snow by late afternoon," he said when the dog sat beside him. "I guess we've got ourselves a boy, Buck."

He reached down and patted the top of Buck's head. "Now, what are we gonna do with him?"

A QUIET SPOT IN THE WOODS
BY DEL GARRETT

The creek at San Jacinto loomed in the distance. From this angle, Juan Ortiz could see it to the north, the rise of the creek bed to the west and the thick patch of trees to the east. They formed a 100-yard triangle with him square in the middle at its base. He had found the spot indicated on the crude hand-drawn map provided by his Uncle Jorge, a colonel in Santa Anna's army.

At sixteen, Juan was a natural scout, calculating directions by the moon and stars at night, by the moss on the trees during the day and by the way the greener shrubs grew over underground water paths. He needed no compass or spyglass, simply the natural lay of the land and his own five senses, plus a gut feeling sometimes when he felt danger in the air. So, his uncle agreed, the boy was the perfect little soldier to carry out the assassination plot.

■ ■ ■ ■

Today was supposed to be perfect for his mission. Juan settled down inside a dip in the earth which would have made a good resting spot for a deer during the hot part of the day. He had an ample supply of shade and a natural elevation for his rifle. He slipped the buckskin cover off his new British Baker rifle and loaded the barrel.

The Baker had proved its value at the Battle of New Orleans, so Santa Anna had outfitted his troops with them prior to marching on the Alamo.

Juan looked first at the creek landing where a few people were starting to show up and again at the line of trees where two men waited and smoked and generally did nothing but sip their morning coffee and talk.

He set a bipod in the moist ground and propped the barrel against it. Satisfied that he was ready, Juan looked at his watch and saw that he had enough time to relax and have a bite of the chicken *torta* his Aunt Rosa had prepared for him. He rolled over and, without disturbing the branches above his head, looked up to see the first flock of geese he'd seen that season pass overhead.

The crystal blue sky had no clouds. It was a perfect day to be in the woods, a perfect day to be alive, a perfect day for getting things done. Juan closed his eyes and fell asleep.

When he awoke, he could hear the sound of voices coming from the creek bank. He pointed his rifle toward the creek. The men he'd seen earlier seemed to be leaving. Juan breathed a sigh of relief. Being asleep, he had not noticed the arrival or departure of the group he had come for. The sound of a horse whinnying drew his attention toward the tree line. He spun the rifle in that direction and looked through the spyglass he carried. Soldiers were setting up tents. Juan studied the men but still could not identify his primary target, General Sam Houston.

He waited. His uncle had urged him to be quiet and be patient, the mark of a good scout or sniper. Excited, as any young person might be with such an important task handed to them, Juan stroked the butt of his rifle as he would a kitten or a pretty *señorita*.

Juan's attention fell upon a large gray stallion emerging from the tree line. The rider, a tall and stout man, and equally as handsome as the horse he rode, popped into view. The soldiers on the ground gathered around the rider and their shouts and arm waving told Juan he had found his target.

"Hola, Señor Houston," Juan whispered. He took aim at the leader of the Texan army and slowly squeezed the trigger of his rifle.

The sound of gunfire echoed throughout the forest. The men at the tree line turned their heads toward the sound and the soldiers there braced themselves with their muskets held at the ready.

Houston looked up at the hilltop. Squinting his eyes against the morning sun, he saw two of his soldiers, his outer perimeter guards, hurrying down the hill toward him.

"Sniper, sir. We got him."

Houston nodded as he dismounted the big gray. He stepped toward a small crop of trees growing by the creek and accepted a cup of coffee from one of the men standing there.

In the distance, following the gunfire, all the animals remained silent. Only one bird flew overhead as Houston looked up and smiled.

Juan Ortiz would not be going home today.

Not So Long in the Tooth

BY ANTHONY WOOD

Long Tooth's pistol lay cocked on the hard dirt floor that smelled of tobacco spit and old bacon grease, but I couldn't reach it. I blinked the dust from my eyes to see my death in his. A wicked grin crept across his jagged face as a small trickle of blood ran down his chin where the long tooth used to be. He struck at the revolver quicker than a rattler. Our hands reached the gun at the same time.

Long Tooth Tom got his name for the wolf-like eye tooth that dropped down an extra half inch. If he glared at you, it'd hang over his right lip like a lawman's hog leg pistol.

I never liked Long Tooth, but I never had to. I avoided running into him, as did everyone who walked the town's lone street. He pushed aside old men, cat-called pretty women, and scared all the children. There was only one way a person could go if Long

Tooth Tom walked out on the street — the other direction.

Long Tooth owned nothing but controlled everything. He even changed the name of the town from Sweet Valley to Long Tooth after he shot the sheriff in the back. He declared the town "law free" except for his law. He didn't know it, but I witnessed the murder.

There was no mistaking the early light of the moon flickering on his tooth that night. Long Tooth knew someone had seen him when I knocked a box over, bolting from my hiding place like a scared rabbit. If he'd known it was me then, I'd be dead now.

Everyone in town knew he killed the sheriff, but were too afraid to speak up. The next day, Long Tooth tacked a fifty-dollar reward sign on a post outside Griffin's Mercantile.

"I want that murderin' scoundrel found!"

Long Tooth watched from a dark alley, trying to figure out who had witnessed the murder. Few stopped to read the reward poster. No one showed up for the fifty dollars.

When my pa died, Mr. Griffin gave me a job in his store stocking shelves, delivering groceries, and sweeping up. The four bits I made each day helped Ma make it week to week. Her sewing money only carried us so far.

Working across the muddy street from the fanciest saloon in town, I witnessed the kind of law Long Tooth offered. It mostly depended on which side of the bed he woke up on that morning, which usually was the wrong side.

Once, a drifter in the fancy saloon across the street joked that Long Tooth was getting a "little long in the tooth." Gray was starting to show a little in his beard, but Long Tooth still had the strength of a bear. In the knife fight that erupted, the drifter felt the full weight of his fatal jest.

While Long Tooth held a knife to the drifter's throat, he sank his long tooth into the man's jugular vein. As the drifter grabbed his throat to stop the bleeding, Long Tooth spit and laughed as the man died on the floor.

"Call me old, will you?" Long Tooth stepped over the drifter's corpse on his way out of the door, but not before he took out the drifter's eye-teeth with his knife. No one did a thing except take the body to the undertaker.

Long Tooth displayed the drifter's teeth on a gold chain he'd taken from my mother not long after my pa died. To this day, she never told me how he got it or why, but I suspected the worst. I couldn't stop thinking about how he'd wronged my mother. I'm sure Long Tooth couldn't stop thinking about the person who saw him murder the sheriff. I never told Ma it was me.

The older I got, the more Long Tooth tried to befriend me. He'd pitch me a nickel or offer to take me fishing. I wouldn't have any of it. I put more distance between us with each passing year. I suspected he might know that I was the witness he'd been looking for all this time. He was patient as a snake, waiting for the opportune time to strike his prey.

Mr. Griffin mysteriously broke his arm the morning I turned twenty-one. Mrs. Griffin asked me to come upstairs to their small apartment after I closed the store that afternoon. When I entered the upstairs bedroom, he asked Mrs. Griffin to get us some coffee.

"Happy birthday!" With his good arm, he handed me a sack tied with a ribbon on it. "I know what happened, son."

I nodded at his arm in a sling. "So do I!"

"I figured as much. I told Long Tooth I wasn't paying protection money any more. He broke my arm and took money out of the register anyway."

I reached into the bag and my jaw dropped. It was the 1851 Navy Colt I'd been eyeing in the store. He knew I wanted it. He even let me fire it out back when I could afford a few bullets. At twenty feet, I could hit all the tin cans lined up on the fence.

Mrs. Griffin hummed up the steps to the bedroom with our coffee. Mr. Griffin shook his head. I stuffed the pistol into my pants and buttoned my jacket. As Mrs. Griffin poured the coffee, I could see the back alley saloon Long Tooth frequented. Cold chills snaked up and down my spine.

Mrs. Griffin handed me a cup. "Sugar?"

"Please."

Mrs. Griffin offered me a spoon. "Would you run the store for us until Mr. Griffin gets back on his feet?"

I didn't have to think about it. "Yes ma'am. I'd be proud to help out."

"Tell your mother to bring her sewing and work in the stockroom if she's a mind to."

"That'd be just fine, Mrs. Griffin." I drained my cup and took the pistol home. I carefully laid it under a floorboard underneath my bed.

I got to the mercantile early the next morning excited to be in charge. Ma brought along her sewing for the day. I opened the door for business just as the blood red sun crept over the fancy saloon across the street. I stepped behind the counter when, of all people, Long Tooth stomped in as my first customer. I jumped, and he saw it.

"Dang boy, you look like you jest been struck by a rattler!" He looked around the store and then his eyes shot straight at me.

"Got it made now, don't you, boy? Or should I call you a man, turnin' twenty-one and all?" I stared into his eyes, wondering how he knew.

"Nothin' gets past me, boy. I know Ole Grif's made you chief store clerk. Who else would do it?"

"What can I get you, Tom?" He didn't like anyone calling him that. He preferred Long Tooth but said nothing about it as customers wandered in.

"Gimme a plug of tobaccy, a box of .44 bullets, and I'll take one of them licorice sticks." He fished a piece out of a jar on the counter and gnawed it with his long tooth. "No need to charge me for this."

I put the bullets and tobacco on the counter. He stretched his neck to look into the stockroom where Ma altered a dress.

"How's yer pretty momma doin'?" I pushed the items toward him with no reply.

Long Tooth snatched up the bullets and tobacco. "You can put this on my bill, boy." My face must've turned red as the blood in my veins.

"No sir, I can't do it. Mr. Griffin is down, but you already know how that happened. He needs his money."

"You sassin' me, boy?"

"Ain't about sassin', Tom. It's about you never payin' up. I've seen the books. You ain't paid in months!"

Other customers drifted our way to catch how this exchange would end. They weren't used to anyone standing up to Long Tooth. He looked left over his shoulder, then right. I was shocked when one man slid a hickory axe handle out of a barrel to study it as he eyed Long Tooth. I gained a little courage when another pulled his jacket back to scratch his ribs, revealing a derringer in his vest pocket.

He didn't move, and neither did I. I wasn't going to avoid Long Tooth Tom. Not this day.

"There now, no need to get upset!" Ma rushed from the back room but stopped short when Long Tooth winked at her, fingering the chain around his neck.

"Good seein' you, ma'am." Long Tooth tipped his hat and scratched his lip with his long tooth. Ma wilted like a rose in the desert heat. She'd always been strong, even when Pa died. But something happened not long after his death — something that made Ma afraid and ashamed. She held that secret close to her chest.

I stepped from behind the counter between Long Tooth and Ma, planting my feet as any good man would when faced with a challenge like this. Long Tooth raised his hand like he was going to hit me. I stepped forward, though my knees wobbled. He could easily slap me across the room, but I didn't back down. The surprised look on his face gave me courage.

"I'll get you, boy, when yer momma ain't lookin'!" I shuddered, but I was in too far to stop now.

"I already got you, Tom! You're just too dang dumb to know it!"

Long Tooth had never lost a word fight. He slunk out of the mercantile like a wounded bear, more dangerous now than ever.

As he pulled the door shut, he winked. "Now I know it for sure, boy." He'd planned all along to smoke me out.

Ma grabbed my arm. "Know what?"

I didn't answer.

There was no mistaking now that Long

Tooth Tom knew I'd seen him murder the sheriff. He would come for me soon.

When Long Tooth left, I felt weak in the knees. Ma sat down hard before she fell down. Lady customers consoled Ma while the men patted me on the back.

Ma wiped her sweaty forehead. "It's what your daddy would've done, son." I appreciated the words, but knew I was alone in this fight . . . just like the sheriff years ago.

"Ma, watch the store. I'll be right back." I sneaked out as Long Tooth stepped toward the ratty back alley bar where he drank and caroused. I knew he'd go there to lick his wounds and gather courage from a whiskey bottle to plan my murder.

I hurried to our small house and pulled up the floorboard that hid my new pistol. I stuck the loaded gun in my belt behind my back under my jacket and returned to the store.

The town lay quiet except for a mule braying down at the livery stable. Funny thing, it sounded a lot like Long Tooth's voice.

The sun set red as the blood ran cold in my veins. Ma sat worrying in the stockroom, fumbling her needle and thimble, unable to concentrate on her sewing. I couldn't concentrate on closing up the store for the picture in my head — Tom's face with that long tooth.

I felt for the pistol in my belt. Pa once told me when our chickens started disappearing one by one, "You can't know when a fox will steal another chicken, but you can know where his den is." The wisdom of my daddy's proverb became clear — don't wait for a fox to come after another bird.

A single coal oil lamp lit two rough oak boards laid across two wooden barrels the saloon proprietor used as a bar counter. My eyes darted about the room over the batwing doors — dang, no Long Tooth.

The owner polished a beer mug. "Who you lookin' for, son?" He stopped polishing when I stepped into the dim light.

"Oh. He's in the outhouse. I wish he'd stay out there. He ain't payin' for his whiskey and his bill is gettin' longer than that ugly tooth of his."

Long Tooth kicked the backdoor open, buckling his gun belt. "Say what, Joe? You makin' fun of my . . . well, what do we have here?" Long Tooth looked me up and down like he was about to skin a hog. "You're a brave boy, ain't you?"

"I don't have to be brave to face the coward who shot a good man in the back."

"It was you all along. I saw that in your eyes today." He squinted. "You have the

137

look of your father!"

The barkeep fell to the floor as Long Tooth pulled his pistol.

I ducked down behind a table, but I was too slow. Long Tooth fired, knocking the pistol from my hand, but not before I pulled the trigger. The bullet ricocheted off a spittoon and struck Long Tooth in the mouth. He screamed, and we both fell to the floor with Long Tooth's revolver between us.

That pistol looked familiar.

Blood dripped down his scraggly bearded chin. With his eyes glued on me, he spit out the long tooth that had made him famous.

"Knew you'd come." Long Tooth eyed the pistol and grinned. I wanted to scream when I glanced at the gun again. "Yeah boy, I'm gonna kill you with your daddy's gun."

I wanted to cry, and I wanted to kill him. I couldn't do both.

Long Tooth tried to fool me like a snake charming a frog as his hand crept toward the weapon. My hand shot at the pistol like a frog fleeing a snake. We reached it at the same time. His fingers slapped the end of the barrel around just enough for me to grab the pistol grip and pull the trigger. Blinding smoke filled the room. I didn't move.

As the smoke cleared, a hoarse voice cried

out, "My tooth's gone, and you got me in the liver, boy. Oh it hurts, finish me!"

I locked eyes with Long Tooth, pursed my lips, and slowly shook my head.

"You made this town too miserable for too long, Tom. Now you're just an old toothless hound that's lost his bite."

Long Tooth reached for my daddy's pistol one last time. I held it steady as I watched the light drift from his eyes.

"Guess you ain't so long in the tooth after all, Tom."

As the town gathered outside, I took my mother's gold chain from Long Tooth's neck and removed the drifter's teeth. I put Tom's long tooth in my pocket and left him dead on the floor.

The next morning, I put the Navy Colt back in the case in Mr. Griffin's store.

I didn't need it anymore.

Now I carry my daddy's pistol on my hip and his silver star on my chest.

"Not So Long in the Tooth" was published in the Winter 2020 issue of *Saddlebag Dispatches* and won a Will Rogers Copper Medallion Award for Western Short Fiction in 2021.

A WILL TO RESIST

BY KIMBERLY VERNON

"Sheriff, there's fixin' to be trouble." The old man stood in the doorway, shifting his weight back and forth and wringing his hat in his hands.

"Why's that, Tuck?" Sheriff Mason looked up from the papers he was studying.

"Old man Crawford done died, and his kin are bound to start feuding again."

Sheriff Tom Mason shook his head. "Surely even they can get along long enough to bury the man."

"I doubt it. Jake Crawford's over at the Brown Jug right now, guzzling whiskey and running his mouth. Mumbling that somebody done killed his grandpa. Says he ain't letting nobody keep him from what's rightfully his. He's pretty worked up."

"Well, Jake Crawford's nothing but a spoiled rich kid who drinks too much and talks even more. I reckon I'd best go over there and try to calm him down." He stood and settled the Stetson on his head, adjusted his gun belt, and strode across the dusty street toward the saloon.

When he pushed through the swinging doors, he immediately saw the young cowboy leaning on the bar, waving a glass in the air and talking just below a shout. He walked up and placed a palm on the bar beside the man.

"Howdy, Jake."

The younger man spun toward him in surprise. "Sheriff! I'm glad to see you. I want to swear out a warrant. That thievin' uncle of mine done killed Grandpa!"

"Jake, I'm sorry about your grandpa." Sheriff Mason put his hand on Jake's shoulder. "He was a good man. But nobody killed him. He's been sick for months, and everybody knew he was dying, including him."

"No, Ray killed him," the cowboy shouted. He jerked his arm away, knocking his glass onto the hardwood floor. "So he could get the ranch. I'll kill that scoundrel before I let him take it."

Sheriff Mason shook his head. "Jake, you can't go around threatening to kill anyone. And you can't be in here yelling and breaking things. Come on, come with me. We'll get some fresh air." He half-pulled, half-led the young cowboy toward the door.

The cool night air brushed their faces, but did little to sober the young man. He continued to mutter about his uncle Ray and the ranch as he stumbled across the street beside the sheriff. When they reached the jail, he realized where they were.

"You arrestin' me, Sheriff?"

"Nope. But I'm gonna let you sleep it off in here before you get into some trouble you can't get out of. Go on and hit the hay. We'll talk in the morning."

The sheriff stepped back onto the sidewalk outside the jail and peered into the shadows between the dimly lighted jail and the bright lights of the saloon. "Tuck? You still around?"

The grizzled old-timer shuffled out of the shadows. "Yep. Right here, Sheriff."

"Tuck, ride out to Jake's mama's place and tell them he's going to sleep in the jail tonight. Let 'em know he's okay, he's not arrested, but he's been pretty deep in the bottle and I'm going to keep my eye on him. If the main house is dark, just tell the foreman at the bunkhouse. He can decide whether to wake her."

"Sure thing, Sheriff. You're awful good to that boy."

"I'm just trying to keep him from starting something while he's drunk that I'll have to clean up later."

"More likely you're trying to get on the good side of his pretty mama."

"What'd you say, Tuck?"

"Nothin', Sheriff. I'll just get going." The old man hurried toward the stable.

The sheriff stared after him a moment, then ambled back inside the jail.

The whole community pressed into the small graveyard to pay respects to Winston Crawford, one of the largest landowners in the area. Ray Crawford, Winston's only living son, stood near the grave surrounded by his ranch hands.

Across the freshly turned earth, a blond woman in a long black dress leaned on the arms of two young cowboys. All three stared at Ray Crawford with hate-filled eyes. Ray tried to ignore the glares from his sister-in-law and nephews, Jake and Joe, as the town preacher droned on.

According to the preacher, otherwise known as the town barber, his father was now in a better place, a beautiful land flowing with milk and honey. Ray felt pretty sure his father would rather be here on his own beautiful land, which flowed with crisp, clear spring water and healthy long-horn cattle. Although one advantage his dad now had was that he no longer had to deal with the three leeches that were staring Ray down.

The preacher wound up a lengthy prayer, and some ladies from the church sang a dirge. People began drifting by, shaking his hand or patting him on the back. He tried to focus on the words they mumbled, but most were meaningless. These people had known his father or had business dealings with him, but none were really friends.

As the crowd thinned, the two nephews and their mother moved closer to Ray. He nodded and spoke. "Janice, how are you?"

"You turned him against us, didn't you? You made him draw up a new will," she whispered low and fast.

"It's a shame you didn't bother to come around when he was alive. He could have told you himself."

Her eyes flashed. "You son of. . . ."

"This ain't the place, Janice." Ray took a step to turn away.

Jake grabbed Ray's arm and jerked. "Don't you walk away when my mother is talking to you."

Ray froze. "Jake, this ain't the place. Now remove your hand."

Jake jerked his arm again. "Or what, you thievin' snake?"

Ray spun and drove his right fist into Jake's jaw, then threw a left cross that landed neatly on the nose of his nephew Joe, who had stepped forward. Janice shrieked.

Jake drew his pearl-handled revolver just as six ranch hands leveled their pistols at him. No one could help but notice their guns were much steadier than Jake's. The remaining crowd backed away.

Ray reached over and snatched the pistol from Jake's hand. "You little piss-ant. You wore your gun to your grandfather's funeral? When are you going to grow up?" He emptied the bullets from the shiny pistol into his palm and slipped them into his pocket. Then he tossed the gun to the ground and strode away. He was as disgusted with himself for being goaded into a fistfight at the old man's funeral as he was at his nephew.

Sheriff Mason removed his hat and knocked. The door swung open and Jake Crawford stood staring with suspicion.

"Jake, I need to speak to your mother."

The young man stood tall and challenged, "About what?"

"That's enough, Jake. Please come in, Sheriff," Janice Crawford said.

"Ma'am, may we speak in private?" Sheriff Mason eyed Jake as the younger man turned red and opened his mouth to object.

"Of course. Jake, leave us."

"But, Mama . . ."

Janice raised her hand and tilted her head. Jake stomped from the room and slammed the door.

"It's about the will, isn't it?" Janice slid her eyes toward him.

Sheriff Mason swallowed and flushed. "Yes. The lawyer is asking you to meet with him and Ray tomorrow. The boys can come, but only if they agree to come unarmed and not interrupt things."

"Ray talked him into changing his will, didn't he?" She pursed her lips into a pout.

"Now, I don't think Ray talked him into anything, Janice. After Jim died, Winston was bound to change the way it read. You can't blame him for that. And your boys haven't exactly been working to reconcile with their uncle Ray."

"Jim's share should belong to me." She raised her voice and stomped her foot.

"Janice, you know better than anyone that Winston Crawford didn't think like that. Just come to the meeting tomorrow. I don't know what they're going to say, but try not to stomp your feet and holler at the lawyer.

That usually don't go too well." He grinned at her.

Janice blushed and smiled. "Good evening, Sheriff. Thank you."

Ray watched Mr. Smithson, his father's lawyer, shuffle papers while waiting for everyone to get seated. Janice entered the room and choose a seat, ignoring him. He'd rather be anywhere else at this moment, but a showdown with Janice and his nephews was bound to happen. He'd tried to warn Smithson, but the poor man didn't know what he was up against. He'd taken the precaution of asking Sheriff Mason to be outside in case things got heated. Jake was a notorious hot head, and Joe was even younger and possibly more foolish.

The lawyer cleared his throat. "Mr. Winston Crawford left very clear instructions, so there is no confusion here today. His ranch, the Rolling C, including all its land and livestock, transfers to his son Ray Crawford."

Janice leaped to her feet. "He had two sons!"

"Yes, ma'am. We're all aware of that. His son, Jim Crawford, preceded him in death, leaving one remaining son."

Ray said, "I'm sorry Jim's dead, but he

made it clear he wasn't a rancher. Daddy tried for years to get him and your boys to learn the ranch. It's hard work. They had no intention of working, so he didn't leave them a cut."

Ray wanted to remind her that instead of staying here and learning how to run the ranch, Jim had to traipse all over the country, gambling on Daddy's money. It was no surprise he ended up shot dead at a poker game. But Ray couldn't bring himself to say those words to her. Even as much as she'd hurt him all those years ago, he couldn't be that cruel. "You backed the wrong horse, Janice," he muttered for her ears alone.

She spun and slapped him in the face.

The room exploded in commotion. Jake and Joe jumped to their feet, shouting and pointing.

Sheriff Mason opened the door and bellowed, "Sit down and hush! Everyone!"

When the noise subsided, Mr. Smithson continued. "Mr. Crawford left funds in the local bank specifically for Janice Crawford, Jake Crawford, and Joe Crawford. He also left the home where they currently live and forty acres surrounding it equally to Janice, Jake, and Joe. He concluded by asking you all to please get along. Are there any questions?"

Jake asked, "How much money's in that bank account?"

Mr. Smithson shook his head. "You'll need to meet with the bank president to get those details."

Ray rose and turned to his nephews. "If you ever decide you'd like to learn the ranch business, I can always find a job for you. Learn the business and then start adding to your spread. It's hard work, but it pays fair."

Jake glared at him. "You can go to He . . ."

Joe grabbed his brother by the shoulder and dragged him toward the door, casting a wary look at his uncle.

Turning, Ray found Janice shooting daggers at him with her icy blue eyes.

"Is this supposed to be fair? We get forty acres and you get how many hundreds?"

"The fact that you don't have a clue is part of the reason, Janice. My father valued hard work and integrity above all else. It broke his heart that Jim and those boys wanted nothing to do with the ranch. Go see the banker. I'm sure Pop took care of you."

She pulled her shawl tight around her shoulders and marched out the door.

Ray finished signing papers for the lawyer, shook his hand, and took his leave. He considered having a drink at the saloon, but

149

thought better of it. His nephews were likely still in town drinking and looking for trouble, and there was no sense in helping them find it. He and two of his trusted ranch hands rode home together.

The following Saturday evening, Ray sat at his desk going over payroll numbers for the hired hands when he heard a knock at the door. Since the cook had already gone home for the night, Ray rose and walked to the door. Expecting his foreman Isaac, he pulled the door wide, but stopped in surprise.

Janice stood on the porch, a horse and buggy tied at the rail. "Hello, Ray. May I come in?"

Her hair flowed from under her hat in curls and cascaded across her shoulders, the gold striking against the blue of her dress. What was she doing here?

He stepped back, holding the door open. "Of course. I'm in the study." He closed the door behind her and followed her into the room. He stepped to his desk and closed the ledger book, then leaned against the desk, waiting for her to speak.

"I came to say I'm sorry. I know I have been dreadful to you, and I apologize. Can you ever forgive me?"

Ray rubbed his hand over his face. "Sure, Janice. I forgive you."

"Oh, good," she gushed, stepping toward him. "I felt terrible about the hard feelings between us."

"No hard feelings. Are you and the boys doing all right?"

"They're about grown and don't need me anymore. But I was just wondering. You know, wondering if there might be, well, something," she stared into his eyes and placed her hand on his chest, "something for me here."

She was very close now, so close he could smell her perfume and feel her breath. Ray felt his heart racing under her palm. This was the only woman he'd ever loved. The same woman who'd stomped his heart twenty years earlier. The woman who'd played brother against brother in her quest to get her hands on the Crawford fortune. The woman who'd chosen fun and excitement over love and respect.

Ray grasped her wrist and gently lifted it from his chest. "No, Janice. There's nothing for you here. That flame went out a long time ago."

"But, Ray . . ." Her blue eyes glistened with tears.

Ray drew a deep breath. He'd rather face

her fury than her tears any day. He pressed his handkerchief into her hand. "Janice, you're still young. And still beautiful. There are men in this town who'd be honored to even be noticed by you. Why, Sheriff Mason practically trips over his boots every time he sees you."

"But it's you I want, Ray," she sobbed.

He took her elbow and gently guided her to the door. As he walked her onto the porch, he told her, "It's the Crawford money you want, not me. It always was, and I'll not fall for that again."

She jerked her arm from his grasp and stomped her foot, then let out a shriek like a mad heifer.

"Isaac!" He shouted to the bunkhouse.

"Yes, sir, Mr. Ray," the foreman answered from across the dooryard.

"Have a couple of the hands escort Mrs. Crawford safely home."

"Yes, sir."

"Goodbye, Janice, and good luck."

ONE ARM OF THE LAW

BY GARY RODGERS

"Jacks, come on out of that jail. Bring whoever the one-armed fellow is with you. There's no need in you two getting hurt over the marshal. We know he's in bad shape, so I'm taking my boy home with me. I'll give you two minutes."

The old man guarding the jail looked at me and grimaced.

"That would be Conner Noland out there. It's his boy, Luke, locked up back there in the cell. Marshal Cates brought him in yesterday for killing a man down at The Thirsty Miner. I can't let him go and I won't let them in here with the marshal. If you want to leave, you can, young man. This really isn't your fight."

Looking over at the marshal being tended to by the town doctor and back at the jailor, I weighed my options. He was right. I didn't know these people, and it really wasn't my fight. But right is right, and I always had a

153

way of getting involved in what was right.

"Jacks, is that what I heard the Doc call you?" He nodded his head. "I guess when I found the marshal out by the tracks nearly beaten to death and decided to help, it became my business. Doc, how's the marshal looking?"

"Not good. He's got several broken ribs and lost a lot of blood. He might even be bleeding inside, I can't tell. I didn't catch your name, by the way."

"That's because I didn't throw it. It's Cory Miller." Then I decided to lie. "The marshal was in bad shape when I found him, but he was still talking. He deputized me before he passed out on the way to town. Jack's, do you have another badge lying around here somewhere? It looks like I'll be helping you keep those men out of the jail."

Doc and Jacks looked at each other before answering my question. I could see they were suspicious of what I had just told them. I would just have to trust it would work itself out.

"There's a badge in the top drawer of the marshal's desk. I've known Marshal Cates for several years now and I ain't ever known him to deputize anyone, especially some stranger." Jacks was keeping his eye on the men outside but letting me know he wasn't sure about my story.

"Maybe the marshal was afraid he wouldn't make it back into town and wanted someone to hold his prisoner. I don't know, Jacks. But I certainly can't leave you here to defend the marshal and hold the jail by yourself."

"If the town folk knew Marshal Cates was going to be okay, they'd be out here running these men out of town. Without him, they don't have enough courage to come outside. So I guess it's you and me, Deputy."

Opening the top drawer, I found the badge and pinned it to my trail dust covered shirt. This wasn't the first time I had worn a badge, but the last time was before the war, before the loss of half my left arm.

"I'm going out there to talk to these men. Bar this door behind me. If anything should happen to me, I recommend you use that scatter gun on Luke back there. If the marshal jailed him for killing a man, then we need to make sure he doesn't walk out of that cell."

I didn't wait to hear Jacks or the Doc's reply. I knew they would argue, and I've learned when there's business needing tended to, it's best to get it done.

Opening the door, I quickly assessed the

location of Conner Noland's men as I walked out onto the boardwalk. They had all taken up positions on the boardwalk across the street that would give them cover. The townspeople had moved inside in anticipation of trouble. I needed to change the circumstances to my advantage. But one of Conner's men was in danger of escalating the situation.

"Would you look at that, boss? The one-armed man is wearing a badge. And two tied-down holsters. Now why in the world would a one-armed man need two guns?" He strolled out into the street, smiling as he began his taunts. "Maybe he plans on taking all of us to jail, boss."

I knew I had to get Conner's attention quickly, before his longhaired hired gun could encourage the others to join him.

"Jacks," I yelled. "If any of these men make any sudden moves, you cut that boy, Luke, in half with your scatter gun. Do you hear me?"

"I hear you, deputy." Jacks answered.

"Curly, get back over here," Conner barked.

I could see Curly wasn't happy with being put on a leash. So, just to keep his attention on me, I winked at him and smiled. "Get back on the porch, boy. Mind your master."

156

He really wanted to make a play for his gun, but didn't. That told me all I needed to know about Conner's hired hands. They might be tough, but they didn't cross the old man.

"Deputy, my men do what I tell them to do. But if I were you, I wouldn't go trying to push . . ."

"I'll do the talking out here, Mr. Noland. I already heard what you had to say. Now you can listen to me."

He wasn't used to being interrupted, and didn't like it. But the threat of Jacks and his scatter gun had gotten his attention.

"You and your men will ride out of town and back to wherever you call home. Your boy will get a fair trial when the judge comes through next week. The marshal should be up and around by then, and he can testify to what he saw happen at the saloon."

"Pa, he's lying to you." Luke's voice came screaming from the jail. "The marshal is near dead in here. Come get me out, Pa."

Curly stepped off the boardwalk and started across the street. I waited to see if Conner would call him back, then I headed for Curly, walking fast, never taking my eyes off of him.

His hand moved to his gun, but I was too

close. Every gunfighter knows when two men are close together, neither one is likely to miss. Then I hit him with a clubbing blow from my hardened right fist, just in front of his left ear. A man gets unusually strong when he only has one arm. He folded like a bad hand at a poker table. Sinking to his knees, his face planted in the dusty street.

It had only taken a few seconds. My right hand wrapped around the handle of the colt as I faced Conner and his men. Several had reached for their guns, but Conner's arms were outstretched, holding them back.

"Mr. Noland, I don't want to die, and I don't want to kill any of your men. I suggest you load Curly up and head home. Your boy won't be getting out of jail today."

The glare of hatred coming from Conner Noland let me know I had made a deadly enemy. His fear of Jacks killing his son was the only thing keeping his men from killing me at the moment.

Conner slowly walked off the boardwalk to stand face to face with me. "Deputy, I'm leaving a couple of men in town to keep an eye on you and on the jail. The rest of us will go back to my ranch for now. If anything happens to my boy, I will burn this town to the ground."

With that, he started for his horse along

with his men while two of them loaded Curly on his horse. As they loaded him, one man turned and spoke.

"I want to give you a piece of advice, Deputy. Leave town today. When Curly comes around, he'll be looking to find you. As for Mr. Noland, nobody shows him up and lives very long. The marshal tried. You see what's happened to him? Folks respected the marshal; they don't even know you." He climbed on his horse, following the rest of the men out of town.

Walking back to the jail, I noticed people coming out of the businesses along the street. Some giving a slight nod or wave to acknowledge their appreciation of how the situation had ended. I nodded back, but kept walking, not wanting any of them to notice the sweat on my forehead.

"You made yourself an enemy out there, Deputy." Jacks was the first to speak as I entered the marshal's office. "That Curly fella is dangerous. He's killed three men since he showed up in these parts. Marshal Cates could never prove he murdered them, but he had his suspicions."

"I've run across the likes of Curly before, Jacks. He'll have to be dealt with soon enough. I just wanted to buy some time without it costing anybody their life today."

"Well, it looks like the marshal's fever may be breaking. So maybe that's a good sign." Doc spoke up, sounding hopeful.

"That last fella talking to you is Gus Malcolm, the foreman at Noland's ranch. He's no gunman, but he's tough as an old hickory. What'd he say to you?" Jacks wasn't satisfied.

"He just told me to watch my back. Curly would be looking to settle our differences when he wakes up. And Mr. Noland doesn't like to be bested. I had that figured out already."

I checked on Luke as he gave me an earful about his pa and how the town would burn if we didn't let him go. I just stared at him till he stopped talking. I didn't have to like him to know I still had to feed him.

"Jacks, where do I go to get all of us some dinner? I'm getting kinda hungry. Last time I ate was last night."

About that time, a train whistle blew a way out of town. I had almost forgotten about the train outside of town.

"Dinner will be here shortly. Emma, over at the hotel, brings dinner when she hears the train coming in."

"Deputy, the marshal is coming around." Doc interrupted.

160

"Doc, where am I?" Marshal Cates whispered.

"You're in your office, Marshal. Deputy Miller found you out by the tracks last night and brought you in."

"Deputy Miller? Who are you . . ."

"Nice to see you feeling better, Marshal. I'm Cory Miller, the man who found you last night. You might not remember too much about it, what with the beating you had taken."

"I remember the beating part, and maybe seeing you. But what's this about being a deputy?"

It was time to confess.

"I told Jacks and the Doc here you had deputized me. Only because Conner Noland and his men were here to get Luke and he was making some serious threats, Marshal."

"You lied to us?" Jacks almost screamed.

"With what he did to get rid of Conner and his men, Jacks, I think a little lie can be forgiven, don't you?" Doc answered.

"Maybe, but he needs to get that badge off now." Jacks still wasn't happy.

"Hold up just a blame minute." Marshal Cates grunted as he tried to sit up.

"Lay down, Marshal. You don't need to be trying to move around." Doc eased the marshal back on his cot.

"Okay, Doc, okay. But this man held off Conner and his men by himself?"

"He sure did and knocked Curly out cold to boot. He didn't even have to pull his gun. Pretty impressive, if you ask me." Jacks was smiling as he told his version.

"Marshal, the whole thing is far from over." I wanted him to know all of it. "Conner left a couple of men in town to keep an eye on the jail. I saw them stop Curly's horse and take him in to the stables with them. I suspect he'll be back here soon."

Jacks and Doc were quiet, since this was news to them as well. But I could see the marshal was putting the pieces together in his head.

"Well, I have two witnesses here to see it, so if you're willing to help, I'm deputizing you now." We shook hands as I nodded my okay. "Now write these names down. I know some of the men who attacked me. Jacks can help you identify them."

I wrote down the names he gave me and it was no surprise Curly was one of them. The marshal was certain there had been six men, but he only knew four of them.

"I was riding out to the Noland ranch to warn them. The man Luke shot has a brother. He'll be looking to get revenge; he's

162

just that kind of man. I don't know who shot me, but it knocked me out of my saddle and then they were on me. Kicking and stomping and clubbing me till I was sure I was dead. I even heard one of them say they thought I was dead."

"I took you for dead when I spotted you last night. But when I rolled you over, you let out a groan. When I saw your badge, I brought you here."

"Deputy, get your sorry hide out here. Me and you got unfinished business." Curly had come to, ready to fight.

"Marshal, it's legal now, so I need to go arrest a man." He nodded as I stood up.

Walking to the window, I could see Curly in the middle of the street. Wisely, he had chosen far enough away to avoid a repeat of our earlier encounter. Looking more closely, I could see the other two men had taken positions on either side of the street. I started for the door, knowing this wouldn't be easy.

"Hold up, Deputy," Jacks stopped me. "Let me go out first with this scatter gun. There are three of them out there. Maybe I can help a little." I nodded my agreement.

Jacks walked out and positioned himself behind the porch post without saying a word. From the door, I could see the other two men looking at each other. The idea of Jacks with a scatter gun wasn't sitting well.

I started talking as soon as I walked out. "Curly, I'm placing you under arrest for the assault on Marshal Cates last night." I kept walking into the street, trying to watch all three men for movement.

"You ain't arresting nobody, Cripple." His hand was on his pistol. "I intend to kill you and then Jacks. After, I'll go in there and finish off the marshal and take Luke back to his pa."

His hand jerked the pistol from the holster; he was fast, but not fast enough. My colt leaped into my hand and bucked before he ever got his pistol leveled. The bullet from my forty-five hit him square in the chest, knocking him backwards. He was dead before he hit the ground. I heard Jacks' shotgun roar and turned on the second gunman just as he fired and missed. I didn't.

I looked and could see Jacks reloading, so I walked to Curly to make certain he was dead. There was no doubt about the one Jacks had shot. The third man wasn't moving.

"Noland!" The shout came from the jail.

As I turned, I could see a man with a rifle. He was emptying it into the jailhouse. I had failed the Marshal. Then I heard the roar of

Jacks' shotgun again as the man seemed to explode in the doorway.

Running back to the jail, I looked inside to find the horrified look on the doctor's face, and Luke Noland was dead in his cell.

"That was the brother of the man Luke killed. He wasn't shooting at me." The Marshal choked.

"I didn't know that, so he's dead now." Jacks had silently walked in behind me.

The sound of horses racing into town filled the air. Jacks and I both ran back out to the street. It was Conner Noland's ranch hands, without Conner Noland. My Colt was still in my hand as they skidded to a stop in front of the jail. Gus Malcolm was leading them.

"Deputy, I don't know what's happened here, but some drygulcher shot Mr. Noland out at the ranch as soon as we rode back in. We followed his trail back to the railroad. We're sure he came back here to Vinita." I could hear the anger in Gus's voice.

"Climb down and have a look, Gus. I think you'll find your killer is dead already. But I have to tell you, he got to Luke while Jacks and I were dealing with Curly and his buddies."

Several of the riders dismounted and walked over to look at the dead body, then peered inside at Marshal Cates. Only Gus walked on inside.

"Marshal, I'm sorry about all that's happened. Luke was a loose cannon and Boss wouldn't hold him accountable. I want you to know none of my regular hands had any part in this." Gus' voice was sincere.

"I know, Gus, and I would just ask your men to let my deputy sort all this out. I would, but it's going to be a while before I can get around."

"Your deputy already proved himself, Marshal. I'll help him any way I can."

"Well, Deputy Miller, you feel like being the law around here until I get back on my feet?"

"I was supposed to be in Kansas City for a position with the Pinkerton Agency. But it can wait. Marshal, I'll do my best." I smiled as I held up my good arm. "I guess one arm of the law is better than none."

"One Arm of the Law" was published in *Saddlebag Dispatches,* Summer 2020.

BUSHWHACKED

BY DON MONEY

"Marshal Rodgers, you surprised me," the woman answered the door out of breath, having just come in the back door moments before from splitting wood. "Is Jimmy not with you?"

The marshal removed his hat. "Mrs. Tate, I don't know how to tell you," he said, averting his eyes, "I don't have the words."

She knew then, this was not a social call. The hat in hand, the look. "Come in." She stepped aside, ushering the marshal in. "I think we can cut the formality, Virgil. Did he suffer?"

The stoic marshal almost broke, "No, ma'am." He looked directly at her. "Emma, that man loved you like no other man could love a woman. Jimmy talked about you without ceasing every ride we went on. Helping people, locking up drunks, leading a posse hunting down outlaws, he always talked about coming home to you."

Emotion washed over Emma. "I know he always looked up to you, Virgil. He said there is no one else he would rather be a deputy for. The last thing he said was that the two of you were riding out to Cross Canyon to look into a report of some men hiding out there. What happened?"

"A group of town folks were concerned about a group of rough-looking men camped out there," the marshal began. "They were afraid they were the no goods that had been reported tearing up the town at Hill Creek. We thought we would ride out and check them out. If they seemed to be troublemakers, we would encourage them to ride a little further on."

Emma knew her husband was an easy-going man, but fiercely protective of the citizens of Harmony Branch. "Go on."

The marshal continued, "There were four of them in camp and we could tell right away they were trouble when one more popped up behind us. They were bush-whackers. The leader in camp laughed as a way of welcome and told us we had bit off more than a couple of local lawmen could handle. They had the drop on us from the jump. No way was either of us riding out of there."

Emma was being drawn into the story.

"The outlaw behind us held a rifle, laughed, and asked if we had any last words," Marshal Rodgers continued the story. "The gang leader chimed in to say them fast before we mosey off to have our way with the town. He could tell that he had struck a nerve with Jimmy, adding, I'll bet you have a real pretty wife."

Emma knew what was coming.

"Faster than I've ever seen anyone clear leather, Deputy Tate had drawn and shot down the man speaking. The man behind us got a round off hitting Jimmy in the back, but he twisted in his saddle and killed the rifleman. The three others in camp opened up on us, but we were faster. I got one and Jimmy got the other two."

Tears began rolling down Emma's cheeks as she clutched at her dress.

"Jimmy fell off his horse. The wound he took was mortal. I don't know how he survived when the bullet hit him. Fighting for home will always trump a coward's play, I reckon. I jumped from my horse and knelt, holding his head as the end came."

The marshal broke, "His last words were 'Tell Emma I love her'."

SNAKEBIT

BY GARY L. BREEZEEL

At the pinnacle of the ridge, Buck Horn raised a weary hand, removed his hat, and wiped his brow. Whew! Another long day's ride. He picked up his canteen and shook it. Empty. "Sorry, Paint, old fella." He patted his stallion's neck. "I reckon we'll both have to hold out until we get to the next waterhole."

The breeze blew Buck's hair into his eyes, but provided no relief from the scorching heat. He twisted in his saddle and surveyed the scene behind him. Beyond the broad valley, the snow-capped Capitan Mountains towered with majestic splendor. Amid the darkening shadows, the sage still managed to turn the floor of the basin a soft purple. The sage's minty scent helped to dispel the too-familiar odors of dust and sweat and horse.

Any other time, he'd have loved nothing more than to sit here and bask in the grandeur, but not now. No time for such trivialities. He refocused his eyes on his backtrail.

Sure enough, a dust cloud arose about two miles back, but smaller than the day before. Most of the posse must have given up and gone home. But not Sheriff Zeb McClaine. He never quit. Not until he got his man, one way or the other. After ten years as a lawman in Snakebite, he'd earned his reputation. The townspeople called him Old Relentless. It was easier to escape Apaches on the warpath than to shake Zeb off your trail.

Buck sighed and eased Paint into a canter. Two days on the run with scarcely any rest got old. He shifted in the saddle and rubbed his back. Despite his fatigue, he could maintain this grueling pace, but his faithful mount wouldn't make it much farther. The chestnut stallion had borne the brunt of the punishment.

He ought to reach the Rio Hondo early tomorrow. Then, he'd circle back through the stream and head for a hidden valley he'd discovered last summer. If he could keep Paint moving for another day and a half, he'd hole up there, rest up awhile, and let his horse graze. Surely, with enough sleep, he'd manage to devise a plan to elude Zeb.

■ ■ ■ ■

Buck awoke after a restless night. Had some sound awakened him? Confounded posse might have spotted his tracks. And have eyes on him even now. He scanned his surroundings. Nothing moved. The sun stood high in the sky, far above the canyon's walls. He should have cleared out at sunrise. He whistled for Paint, gathered his bedroll, and broke camp. If only he hadn't overslept, he'd have made it to his valley by noon, and they'd never have found him.

No time for breakfast. He'd have to make do with jerky while he rode. Good thing he'd filled his canteen before he bedded down.

Buck guided his mount onto an antelope trail he'd spied the previous evening. In response to a slight tug on the reins, Paint followed the track up and over the canyon's rim. A shot rang out and kicked up dust six feet behind him. Heavy caliber. No doubt, the buffalo gun carried by Shep Butler, the best tracker in New Mexico Territory. Zeb's right-hand man on a manhunt.

Too bad Buck didn't have a dog to kick. His ten-mile trek through the river hadn't fooled Old Relentless, at least not for long, even though he'd ridden out of the water onto solid rock. Nobody could track over solid rock. Yet, somehow, he still had company. Were those guys human? He sighed. No hope now to hide out in his valley and let his horse rest.

At Buck's flick of the reins, the faithful steed leaped into a gallop. Before Shep would have time to reload the single-shot Sharps, they rounded a mammoth boulder, safe for the moment. How fortunate that Buck hadn't bothered with breakfast. He'd have been a goner for sure. Shep, the bloodthirsty cuss, fired first and asked questions later, regardless of Zeb's orders.

Buck slowed Paint, gave him his head, and allowed the horse to pick his way down the rocky incline. But when they reached the level floor of the next canyon, they raced on.

He needed to put more distance between himself and the posse. He hadn't dreamed up an escape plan that made sense, except to try to stay ahead of Zeb until he crossed the border in three or four days. Not his best-thought-out strategy. The overnight stop had given Paint a much-needed respite, but hardly enough for a days-long run for the border.

How unfair that circumstances forced

Buck to go on the run. All his life, he'd been snakebit. He couldn't help that his mother died giving birth to him in the Buckhorn Saloon. Or that they'd named him after the disreputable joint, since nobody knew Goldie's last name. At least Blackjack O'Leary let the other girls raise him when the good citizens of Snakebite wanted no part of him. Still didn't after all this time. So, at twenty-three, Buck worked at the Buckhorn. He'd never left. Until this mess. Cursed luck. Even the rundown saloon seemed like paradise after this.

After another full day's ride, Buck began his descent of the south slope of Blanco Pass, the landscape as barren and desolate as any place he'd ever seen. With his bandana, he wiped the sweat from his face. Both he and his mount had about reached the end of their rope. Paint's chest heaved with each breath, while Buck slumped in his saddle.

He gave Paint a gentle kick, and the valiant steed began his descent. About a third of the way down, the horse stumbled and slid sideways. Buck jerked up straight. *Confound it.*

In his fatigued state, he'd failed to spot the loose shale on the slope. Paint lost his footing, fell to his knees, and rolled over. Buck jumped clear, but when he hit the ground, pain shot through his temple. Then all went black.

When he came to, night had fallen. A half-moon hovered above the ridge. He pushed himself to a seated position. Everything spun round and round. As the world slowed to a stop, the cry of an animal in agony rang out from below. He struggled to his feet, then alternately staggered and slid toward the sound. No mean feat on a forty-five-degree grade. His horse lay on one side, head tossing to and fro.

"Easy, boy, let me check you out." The stallion settled enough to allow Buck to approach. He ran his hands over Paint's forelegs. Both broken. Just as he expected. "Sorry, old pard, I can't risk a gunshot." With tears in his eyes, he pulled his buck knife out of its sheath and, with one quick thrust, sliced his best friend's jugular.

Noon found Buck well on his way down the mountainside. He'd left everything except his rifle, canteen, and the last two strips of jerky. His weariness after days on horseback paled by comparison to the fatigue of a half-day's hike in the blazing sun. He'd stopped often for rest and to quench his thirst. For all the good it did him.

He turned and gazed toward his backtrail. No sign of the posse, but they couldn't be far behind.

Long before dusk, all hope of escape fled. Yet, he refused to give up and let them hang him for a crime he didn't commit. He'd die of exhaustion first — he licked his cracked lips — or thirst.

As the sun set, he stumbled on a small spring that bubbled out of a cleft in the rock face. He drank his fill and plunged his head into the pool below. Cool and refreshing. Too exhausted even to refill his canteen, he slogged over to a nearby patch of grass and dropped to the ground. Before full dark, he lay down where he sat and passed out.

At a sharp pain in his side, Buck jerked awake. He rubbed his ribs and opened his eyes to the gray light of early morning. Beneath a battered black Stetson, piercing blue eyes in a leathery, sunburned face stared down at him. A face he knew all too well. But the six-gun pointed between his eyes captured and held his attention.

Zeb kicked him with the toe of his boot. In the same place.

"Ouch!"

"Wake up, kid. You've led me on a merry

chase. It's a rough trip back to Snakebite. Longer, 'cause we'll be ridin' double."

Buck sat up and glanced around. "Where's Shep?"

"Sent him home. Don't cotton to killin' a man when it ain't necessary. Besides, I didn't need a tracker no more. Since you lit out the other day after gettin' shot at, you left a trail a blind tenderfoot could follow."

"Zeb, why not let me go? No one would know."

"Cain't do it. I always liked you, boy, but I've gotta take you back to stand trial."

"But they'll hang me for sure. And I didn't kill Blackjack."

"You'll have a chance to tell your story."

Buck's chin dipped to his chest. "Who'll listen to a nobody who grew up in a saloon?"

"I cain't do nothin' 'bout that." The sheriff reached down and helped Buck to his feet. "Come on. Let's git goin'."

Two nights later, the two sat beside a campfire. Crickets chirped. The nearby creek gurgled. A coyote howled in the distance. The scent of wood smoke filled the air. With a bright canopy of stars overhead, the night would have been restful but for the circumstances. Zeb held out a tin cup. "Coffee hits the spot. Sure you don't want some?"

Buck shook his head, eyes downcast. "I just want you to let me go. I'll leave the territory and never come back. I promise."

"Nope. I've got a duty to them that elected me."

"But you'll be helping them hang an innocent man."

"I'll do what I can, boy, but the evidence is agin' you." He glanced at the flames. "Reckon I'll have to tie you up again before I bed down. Take it easy while I rustle up some more firewood." He stood and disappeared into the darkness.

Moments later, a telltale rattle sounded, followed by a curse and a gunshot. Soon after, Zeb returned, shaking his left hand. "Hurts like blazes. Bent over to pick up a log. Blasted rattler got me."

Buck clambered to his feet. "Come over by the fire." He took Zeb's hand and held it near the flame. Sure enough, two puncture marks dotted the back of his hand. "He got you, all right."

"Well, boy, reckon you got yer wish. I cain't bring myself to shoot you in cold blood. So, I guess all you gotta do is wait around 'til I cash my chips. Then, you'll be free."

Buck stared into the fire. As Zeb said, this might be his last chance to escape the noose. But if he let the man die when he had the ability to help him, he'd become a murderer for real and deserve to hang. No time to dither. Every minute counted. If he hesitated, Zeb would meet his maker.

"Sit here where there's more light, so I can see what I'm doing." Buck removed his bandana and wrapped it around Zeb's wrist. Then, he pulled a small stick from the stack of firewood, tied the loose ends of the neckerchief to it, and twisted it tight. "Now, give me the knife on your belt."

Zeb slid the blade from its sheath and handed it to Buck, who made an X-shaped incision over the bite marks, placed his mouth over the cut, sucked as hard as he could, and spit the poison into the flames. He repeated this procedure over and over. By the time he finished, Zeb's hand had begun to swell.

Next, Buck searched the sheriff's saddle-bags. He took out the dirty shirt, washed it in the stream, and spread it out near the fire. "When it's dry, I'll make bandages to cover your wound. Wouldn't want it to get infected."

For four days and nights, Zeb raved with fever. His hand and forearm swelled to twice their normal size. Buck nursed him to the best of his ability. Compresses of cool water on the injured sheriff's forehead helped keep his temperature down. Buck killed a rabbit with Zeb's Winchester, made broth, and spoon-fed his patient to get some nourishment into him.

At dawn of the fifth day, the sheriff's brow had cooled to the touch. With Buck's help, he managed to sit up and spoon a small helping of beans into his own mouth. By the following morning, his color had returned.

Zeb rolled over and faced the campfire. "Buck, thank you for savin' my life."

Buck sat Indian-style near the fire. "You'd have done the same for me."

"True, but you had good reason not to. No murderer would do what you did. What happened? Tell me your side of the story. You know, witnesses saw you leanin' over Blackjack's body."

The flames flashed yellow, orange, and red as Buck gazed into them. After a moment, words poured out. "I cleaned up the saloon after closing and left by the back door, as usual. When I started down the alley toward the street, I saw Blackjack lying curled up on one side. Kneeled beside him to find out if he needed help, but it was too late. Blood had soaked his clothes and pooled all around. I didn't see a knife until later when I ran past it near the street."

"Where we found it." Zeb leaned forward. "Why'd you run if you didn't do it?"

"Somebody took a shot at me. I had to vamoose or get killed. Bullets don't take the time to ask questions."

Zeb nodded. "Makes sense. I heard a gunshot before I got there." His penetrating gaze bored into Buck's eyes, the same way he studied his opponents at a poker table to detect a bluff. "Do you have any evidence you didn't do it?"

"He had a stab wound in his chest. With so much blood, the killer couldn't keep from getting it all over him. I still have on what I wore the night of the murder. Do you see any bloodstains on my clothes?"

"No, but how can I be sure you didn't change?"

"No time. You saw me run down the street, jump on my horse, and hightail it out of town. Took only what I kept packed in my saddlebags. Left my spare shirt behind when I had to hoof it. You found it, didn't you? With Paint's carcass?"

"I searched your saddlebags. Found your clean shirt." Zeb rubbed his chin. "Dog-gone it. I reckon you're right."

"Does that mean you'll let me go?"

The sheriff laid a hand on Buck's shoulder. "No, son, I still have to take you back. It's my duty, but I'll do whatever I can to clear you. Make sure the judge and jury understand what we just discussed. I think I can convince 'em, but you'll have to trust me."

"I do trust you." Buck nodded and swallowed hard. "You've always been a straight shooter."

"Good. I need another day's rest, but bed down early. We leave at sunup."

"Snakebit" was previously published in *Frontier Tales,* Issue #148, January, 2022.

The Last of Jackson Simms

BY RHONDA ROBERTS

"Sheriff Rawlins. It's never a good day to see you at my door. What's my husband done this time?"

"Mrs. Simms —"

"Don't you 'Mrs. Simms' me. Just spit it out. What's he — wait . . . is Jackson *dead*? He's dead, isn't he? My God. I've been expecting that news every day for the last ten years. Now that it's here, I, I can't decide whether I'm angry, grief-stricken, or just plain old relieved."

"Constance."

"Don't you 'Constance' me either, Henry Rawlins. How did he die? Did the town give him the lynching they've been itching for? Or did you finally kill him?"

"I didn't kill Jackson."

"And why should I believe you?"

"Because half the town saw it happen."

"Then who did it? Who killed my husband? Some gunslinger that came in on the

183

noon stage? Anyone in town would have done it, if they could have. You know what a mean-spirited, worthless brute he was. But nobody in this God-forsaken place besides you could have bested Jackson Simms in a fair gunfight. Unless some spineless nobody shot him in the back."

"He wasn't shot in the back. It was a fair fight."

"Who did it? Who killed the fastest gun in the territory?"

"Billy Joe Wilder."

"Billy? Billy Joe Wilder, the cattleman's son? I've taught him in school since he could barely walk. He can't be more than thirteen years old!"

"He's 12."

"You're telling me a 12-year-old boy killed Jackson Simms in a fair fight?"

"He was highly motivated."

"What do you mean by that?"

"Jackson had been drinking. He wasn't drunk, just that brand of mean he got when he had a couple whiskeys in him."

"He was always mean, and he always had a couple of whiskeys in him."

"Jackson busted the barkeep over the head with a bottle. Someone ran and got Doc Brownley, and Doc's daughter Sarah came with him. She and Billy Joe have known each other all their lives. They were crossing the street as Jackson barged out of the saloon. He punched Doc, grabbed Sarah by the hair, and started dragging her into the alley. You know what would've happened next. There were plenty of folks watching, but none of them willing to stop Jackson. Except for Billy Joe. He told Jackson to stop, but he just laughed. Jackson shoved Sarah aside and went to draw his gun. Billy Joe grabbed a bystander's shotgun and fired."

"Are you going to arrest Billy Joe?"

"Do you want me to?"

"The last thing I'd want is for Billy Joe Wilder to die for ridding the world of a vicious, drunken animal."

"Constance, I'm so sorry."

"For what? For me making the wrong choice all those years ago? You tried to tell me. But I wouldn't listen. Back then, he was handsome, charming, and wild, and I fell for it all. As soon as we married, he started lying, cheating, and beating me. One thing's for certain: I'll never mourn the last of Jackson Simms."

Ambushed

BY KIMBERLY VERNON

The rifle shot echoed through the valley and Rolland saw his partner, Tuck Cruise, jerk forward in the saddle. Tuck tumbled from the saddle and sprawled on the leaves, a stain spreading across the back of his shirt. Tuck's horse bolted away.

Rolland spun his horse, sliding his rifle from its scabbard. He scanned the area behind them but couldn't see anyone. Seeing movement in the trees to his right, he fired. In the rocky, wooded terrain, he didn't know if he faced one or a dozen. He jumped to the ground and dragged Tuck behind a boulder for cover. "Hang on, Tuck."

Tuck tried to speak but coughed instead, blood mixing with the spittle.

As Rolland dashed out and reached for his horse's reins, another shot rang out. The horse jerked his head and galloped away. Rolland dove back behind the rock. He'd worry about the horse later.

Another shot rang through the valley, hitting nearby rocks. Rolland rose from his hiding place and fired toward the wooded hillside the shot came from. Ducking back behind the rocky outcropping, he hurried to reload.

The two sides exchanged several more shots, then quiet fell over the valley. For several minutes, the only sound was Tuck's ragged breathing. Rolland peeked around the edge of the rock, but couldn't see anything.

Rolland climbed up the side of the boulder they were behind to see if he could locate the enemy. He'd reached about six feet off the ground when a stabbing pain hit his leg right below his knee. Unlike any pain he'd ever felt, he knew immediately something was terribly wrong. Pushing himself away from the rock, he saw the rattlesnake on the ledge where he'd planted his knee, coiled to strike again. Unable to catch himself, he fell backwards to the rocks below.

Rolland heard what sounded like an Indian war cry and another rifle shot. He heard a scream, but it may have been his own. He tried to move, but the sky and treetops above him spun. Then all was black.

Rolland's eyes opened in tiny slits. He

could see a campfire lighting the darkness. He was wrapped in buffalo fur. His head pounded and his swollen tongue felt glued to the roof of his mouth. He must have moaned, because a figure rose from near the fire and slowly knelt beside him.

At first, Rolland thought it was Tuck, then he remembered Tuck getting shot. He'd been in bad shape. He tried to turn his head to see if Tuck was nearby, but the slightest movement set his head spinning.

The man kneeling over him had bushy gray hair and a matching beard. He gently lifted Rolland's head and pressed a canteen to his lips. "Howdy, Marshal. Drink a bit of this. If it stays down, we'll try some food."

Rolland gulped greedily until the man pulled the canteen away. "Slow."

Rolland swallowed and paused. Every part of his body hurt, but his left leg felt like it was on fire. "Who are you? Where am I?" The words came out as a croak.

"I'm Biggs. Glad to see you're feeling better."

"I'm not sure about that. I'm feeling pretty rough. What happened? How'd I get here?"

"I reckon a Comanche hunting party interrupted the gun fight you and your friend were losing. I brought you to my

188

camp. You got a couple of nasty rattler bites, but I got you fixed up now." Biggs poured some water from a kettle over the flame into a cup.

"Tuck? My friend?"

Biggs shook his head. "I'm sorry. He was dead when I found y'uns. I buried him."

Rolland closed his eyes. He was so tired. "Thanks. How long have I been here?"

"This is the fourth day. You've mostly been out, but when you woke you was talking out of your head with fever. Here, sit up and drink this." Biggs helped him sit up and pushed a roll of hides behind his back before handing him the cup of hot liquid.

Four days. That put him gone from Fort Smith almost two weeks. No telling how long before he could get back. Rolland eyed the murky greenish color in the cup and sipped. He scrunched his face.

"It ain't supposed to taste good," Biggs laughed. "It's just supposed to keep you alive. Fights the poison and helps with the pain, too."

"I'll drink it, then." Rolland drank a long pull from the cup. He reached out and touched the compress of damp leaves covering his left leg. His breeches were cut right above the knee, and the lower leg was twice the size of the right. He drained the cup

189

without another word.

"It was the breeches or the leg. Figured you'd choose the same."

"Yeah. Obliged."

"You think you could eat? I got some rabbit stew warming."

Rolland closed his eyes, as weak as a newborn kitten. There must be something in the tea to make him sleepy. "I think I'll rest a bit first."

When he opened his eyes next, it was daytime. He wiggled until he was able to sit up without causing too much pain in his leg. Looking around, he saw he was under a small overhanging rock, almost a cave. Bundles of pelts were stacked against the back wall. The campfire had settled to coals. His rescuer was not in sight, but had left a canteen within reach.

Rolland drank deeply and felt his stomach rumble. Now he was hungry. He could hear water running over rocks somewhere nearby, and remembered the man had said the camp was on the Poteau River. Rolland tried to put together what he knew of the area to figure out how far he was from home, but he couldn't. He'd never been this far south into Indian Territory. Tuck had been the one with the knowledge of the territory.

190

Thinking of Tuck reminded him he'd have to tell Tuck's family what had happened. If he made it back. Now that he was thinking clearer, he tried to piece together the events. He recalled hearing the shot. A long-range rifle shot. The second shot came enough later Rolland felt it had been a single shooter. Who would open fire on federal marshals in the middle of the wilderness? And how did Biggs happen to find them? Could Biggs be the shooter? If so, why not leave him to die? It was doubtful, but he needed to find out a little more about this Biggs, and see what kind of weapon he carried.

The sound of someone approaching interrupted Rolland's thoughts. He felt around searching for his gun belt, but found only the canteen. His eyes landed on his rifle, with his coat and pistol, laying out of reach on the opposite side of the fire. He fought to keep his nerves out of his face as Biggs entered the camp carrying a shotgun and a skinned rabbit.

"Hey, you're looking better, Marshal. You ready for some grub?"

"Sure am."

Rolland watched the man move about, stoking up the fire and putting a pot on to heat. With smooth, relaxed movements, he skewered the rabbit and set it over the flames.

"I figure you can eat the stew from yesterday. I'm going to braise this rabbit, but I'd be leery of you eating something that rich after being empty for so long. If the pain is bad, I'll steep you more tea."

"You seem to know what you're doing. How'd you learn doctoring?"

"I've had my share of bites, cuts, and injuries out here. Learned some from the natives, remembered some stuff from my grand-pappy, and experimented some. I've managed to keep myself alive and mostly well for a long time now."

"You live alone out here?" Rolland wanted to get a feel for the man's character, and keeping him talking would help.

"Mostly. Had a wife for a few years until she passed of the fever. Been alone ever since. I see traders a few times a year when I deliver my furs. Pretty much avoid anybody else." Biggs passed him the pot of stew.

"Any idea who was shooting as us?" He took a bite, then another. The rabbit smelled wonderful, but the stew was pretty darn good.

"There's some traffic through here; people running from something, mostly. Were you chasing someone?"

That didn't really answer the question. "Not chasing, but we'd heard a particular pair of outlaws had holed up outside Tali-hina. We followed the railroad down and looked around, but had no luck. We were heading back north, hoping to pick up their trail through the mountains. You see anybody suspicious?"

"Any outlaws passing through here would be left alone as long as they did the same. I keep to myself."

"Then why help me? I'd be dead of snake-bite if you hadn't rescued me."

"I seen the star on your chest. I know the kind of man it takes to wear one. That kind of man don't deserve to die in the wilder-ness with no respect."

Rolland met his eyes. "Thank you."

By day six, Rolland felt stronger and more clear-headed. "I need to figure out how to get home. I have nothing to pay you, but if you can help me get back to Fort Smith, I'll get you a reward. You have my word." He limped across the width of the camp and back, stretching and testing his leg.

"Marshal, I don't want your money. And I can't go marching in to Fort Smith, or Pawnee, or anyplace else."

"You got a horse?"

"I got Rascal, my pack mule. He's old and slow like me, but he's surefooted and fearless. We can get you to the nearest train station. It's two days from here, probably three in your condition."

Rolland straightened. "Let's go at daylight."

Biggs shook his head. "Hold up, now. I need a couple of days to run my traps and get ready. And you could use a few more days of healing. This ain't no stroll we'll be taking. It's steep and rocky. We'll leave in three days."

Rolland wanted to object, but he was at the man's mercy. Biggs had saved his life, and was willing to put himself out further to help him get started for home. He smothered his impatience.

Biggs had been right. The trail snaked through the mountains and travel was slow. They made camp before dark the first day, and Rolland was tired to the bone. This was going to be harder than he'd thought.

"I'd give five hundred dollars for a horse."

Biggs chuckled. "You don't have five hun'erd dollars. And ain't no horses around, anyway." He stirred the fire and added a few long pieces of wood.

They had finished eating the jerky and

biscuits they'd packed when they heard rustling in the bushes. Rolland slid his pistol out and held it near his side.

Biggs grabbed his shotgun. "Who's there?"

"Put that gun down, Trapper. I got no score to settle with you. But the Marshal's coming with me." A man stepped from the trees, his rifle pointed toward the camp.

Biggs lowered the shotgun slowly. "Saves me a heap of trouble," he mumbled.

The armed man glared at Rolland. "Show your hands, Marshal."

Rolland released his grip on the pistol, leaving it on the blanket beside him out of sight, and lifted his empty hands.

"I was going to kill you, Marshall, like I killed your buddy Cruise. But I wanted you to know who I was. Name's Tom Jackson. You put my boys in jail. But I been thinking on it, and I've decided I'll drag you in and trade you for my boys' freedom. Now get up nice and slow."

Rolland, injured, stiff, and exhausted from the day's travel, struggled to stand, grunting with the effort.

While Jackson's attention was on Rolland, Biggs grasped the end of the long stick he'd placed into the fire. He jerked it upward, sending coals and flames into Jackson's face. The man stumbled backwards. Biggs grabbed the shotgun and fired. The blast blew him into the trees, his body sprawled in the underbrush.

At the commotion, Rolland scrambled to his knees and clutched the pistol, eyes searching for any movement. "There may be more."

Biggs circled the camp, searching nearby in all directions for signs of anyone else. He returned a few minutes later, leading a sorrel mare. "I reckon you owe me five hun'erd dollars," he said with a grin.

After unsaddling the mare and securing her with the mule, they settled back at the fire. Biggs took a pan of water off the fire and poured some into a mug, then stirred. "Here, drink this. It'll ease the pain and help you rest. We'll take shifts. I don't like how easy he got up on us. I'll wake you in a few hours."

Rolland swallowed the bitter brew. "Tomorrow'll go easier."

Biggs shook his head. "I hope. Rest, Marshal."

Rolland woke sometime later to Biggs shaking his shoulder. The moon had set and stars dotted the sky.

"Keep the fire up." Biggs stretched out on his bedroll and was snoring almost before Rolland could get up.

Rolland stretched, working the kinks out of his legs and shoulders. He walked over and scratched the mule behind his ears, then stroked the mare. Returning to the fire as quietly as he could, he added a log and settled on a stump.

He tried to think about the upcoming day's travel, but his knowledge of the area was scarce. He'd lost track of how long he'd been gone, and could only guess how much longer it would take to get home. He missed his family.

Before dawn, he started coffee and packed up his bed. He woke Biggs and handed him a cup of the strong black liquid. "Let's get started."

They were on the trail in minutes and made much better time with Rolland atop the horse. Biggs was still walking, his mule packed with camp gear and furs. But a healthy man can cover a lot more ground than a weak, injured one.

By afternoon, they were out of the biggest mountains, and the trail merged with a road. Biggs stopped and wiped his face. "This road will take you into Red Oak before dark. You can trade that horse at the mercantile for a ticket and probably a bed for the night. If I was you, I'd slip that star in my pocket and be a no-name traveler until I got closer to Fort Smith."

"You're not coming?"

"I got no business in Red Oak."

Rolland offered Biggs his hand. "I can never repay you."

Biggs shook his hand. "No need. Just get home alive." He turned and led the mule back up the trail.

Rolland watched until they were out of sight, then turned and kicked the mare into a trot.

Jo's Burden

BY ELLEN E. WITHERS

It wasn't fair. Had Josephine been lucky enough to be the second child born into the Brotherman family, she'd have ridden off to Denver with Papa. Instead, saddled with the responsibilities of the oldest child, she watched twelve-year-old Buck toss his bedroll and saddlebags on his horse. The responsibility of taking care of Frank and the farm fell to her, and she resented it. It wasn't fair. Not fair at all.

"I'm the better rider and a better shot with the rifle than Buck!" Jo wailed when Papa made the announcement, stomping her foot to emphasize her words.

Edward Brotherman nodded his agreement with her assessment. "That's why you're the one who has to stay home, Josephine. I can't make such a long trip without knowing Frank and the farm will be taken care of. Buck can't do it all by himself."

"But there's nothing to taking care of Frank. Buck can do that and still get to all the chores. I admit he's not much of a cook, but I could make some things ahead, to tide 'em over."

He shook his head 'no.' "I considered it, but Frank'll be better off with you and the same goes for the farm." He looked at her with blue eyes filled with sympathy. "Without us around, Buck would go fishing and hunting with nary a thought for all the work needing done around here."

She found no reason to disagree with his logic. Papa was always getting after Buck for his lack of responsibility.

"Now Josephine, I know how much a trip to the city can mean to a young lady, especially since you've been laden with caring for this family since we lost your mother." He slid his arm around her shoulders. "But I couldn't sleep a wink on the road from worrying about everything if Buck was left in charge." Without another word, he'd disappeared out the door.

She knew she'd lost and didn't bother to bring up the subject again.

Two weeks later, she stood barefoot in the soft dust near the corral, watching Buck and her father ride their horses down to the main road with Clovis, their mule, loaded with supplies and trailing behind them. As they made their way, Clovis fought the load he was forced to carry. Jo knew just how he felt. She also fought the load she was forced to carry, unable to overcome her resentment about being left behind.

Papa twisted in his saddle and waved at her and Frank. She waved in response, but refused to smile. Five-year-old Frank, on the other hand, jumped up and down as he waved to Papa. Then he began prattling about nothing, his own bare feet running circles around her while their dog, Herman, made sport of chasing him.

She saw Papa turn toward the cross on top of the hill. He was saying good-bye to Mama. Tears stung her eyes.

The hot sun beat down on her bare head and the knot in her stomach grew bigger. She was stuck here doing the same old chores she did every day, with Papa and Buck's chores to do now, too. Time was gonna drag by. She'd better get busy; might help her forget the hurting in her stomach.

Skirt in hand, she headed for the barn. She pulled on her barn boots to tackle a few chores. "Frank?" she called. "Come feed the chickens."

He loved the chickens, although she was sure the chickens didn't feel the same way about Frank. It was the only chore he could carry out alone, and luckily, it kept him busy while she worked.

When she'd finished, she found him swinging back and forth on the middle rung of the corral fence. While she admonished him for chasing the chickens, she reached through the gate and rubbed the soft muzzle of their donkey, Skeeter.

"Jo?" Frank popped up his blonde head. "How long they gonna' be gone?"

"How about we make a calendar tonight? Just like the one we made for Christmas and you marked off each day. Would you like that?"

"Do I get to do the marking?"

"Yes."

"Yippee!" His yell carried so much excitement it scared Skeeter into a trot.

It surprised her how quickly the days passed. They fell into a rhythm that agreed with both of them. With only two to cook for, meals didn't take much time out of the day. Every evening, they marked the calendar for Papa and Buck's return. It didn't take long for Frank to figure out the more he helped her, the quicker he could do what he liked and he stepped up his assistance. She struggled to be patient when he helped with chores and he surprised her with the sense of pride he felt in his accomplishments.

After nearly three weeks had passed, he called out from his bed one morning. "Jo? Would this be our fishing day?"

His question made her chuckle. She stirred the pan of oatmeal and replied, "Yes, Mr. Smarty."

With a glance up at the loft, she saw he stood in his nightgown looking down at her; hair swirled wildly atop his head.

"Have ya' milked Sally?" he asked.

"Not yet."

"Can she wait for me to help?"

"She can if you hurry."

Within seconds, he'd changed clothes and scooted down the ladder. He pointed to the steaming cereal and said, "Let's do Sally now, while that's cooling. Come on, Jo!" He grabbed her hand and tugged her to the front door.

With a laugh, they raced to the pasture and herded Sally to the barn. He got the bucket off the nail while she placed the milking stool next to Sally. Then he turned to watch the barn cats hovering outside the stall, hoping for a possible squirt of milk.

When she'd almost finished milking, including the cats' reward, she traded places with him. Sally was patient with him as he worked to make a stream. Having practiced this twice a day for several days, he was getting the stream pretty regularly. Sally stopped dancing away as his skill improved.

With his face drawn into concentration, she realized this was the right thing to do for him. They'd been treating him like a baby since Mama died, and now he was ready to grow up.

"You've got it now, Frank."

"Yep," he replied, a bit distracted, as he kept his mind on his work.

Once they were back at the table for their cold oatmeal, she complimented him on his hard work. "I'm sure I wasn't anywhere close to your age when I learned to milk."

"You mean, you was older than me?"

"*Were* older than me," she corrected. "I was maybe six or seven."

"Are you pulling my leg?"

A smile lit his face, and she noticed his cheeks seemed quite rosy with pride. "Did you get hot milking Sally?"

"Nope." He looked down and pushed his oatmeal in circles in his bowl.

She reached across the table and touched his cheek. It seemed warm. "Are you sick?"

He looked up at her and grinned. "Naw, I guess I got hot after all." Scooping a big bite in his mouth, he declared through the oatmeal, "Let's go fishing!"

"Let me change first."

It was nigh onto impossible for her to go fishing in a dress, so she put on a work shirt and an old pair of Buck's trousers. Since turning seventeen, it wasn't fitting for her to wear men's trousers, but who would know if she did? Their closest neighbors were the Pritchards, and they were several miles away.

They hiked to their pond carrying their cane poles, some string, and a can of worms. Herman trailed behind them, gathering scents along the path. They heard him howl at some critter and, while it made Frank clap his hands with delight, it made her sorry she hadn't brought the rifle. They could've had rabbit or squirrel stew tonight. She knew going fishing didn't guarantee a fish would be in the fry pan that evening.

Within a couple of hours after settling down on the bank, both had caught a fish big enough to eat. Once the sun rose in the sky, they didn't get as many bites, but remained there. It was nice to relax and enjoy doing nothing for a while. Frank began to hum a tune Papa liked to hum. It made her hanker for Papa and, although she didn't like to admit it, she missed Buck, too.

Herman bayed at another critter and scampered off. Then she heard a sound that closely matched Herman's, but it came from Frank. It was a deep cough, the kind of cough that made her head snap away from the dog, toward her little brother. It sounded rattling and wet.

She'd heard a cough like that before. It brought back memories she'd pushed away a long time ago. Just the thought of her little brother suffering the same fate made her stomach twist into a knot.

She took a long look at him and noticed his face was much more flushed now than it had been this morning. *I should have paid more attention to his red cheeks at breakfast!* He was staring at his cork floating in the water with bleary eyes. Her stomach twisted tighter.

She scrambled to her feet. "Frank, it's time for us to head on home," she said, fear peppering her voice.

Normally, he would have fussed and sputtered about leaving, but today, he just pushed himself to his feet and produced another nasty cough in the process.

He looked like he might tump over. She rushed to him, dropping her pole on the bank and leaving their string of fish forgotten in the water. When she reached him, she put her hand on top of his head and horror painted her face as the heat of his fever seared her hand. *This is bad. Real bad.*

"Why didn't you tell me you were sick?" She bent down level with his face.

His brown eyes, underlined with ominous circles, looked into hers and filled with tears.

"Don't cry Frank, I'm not mad at you. I'm angry at myself for not seeing you weren't feeling right. We gotta' get you home!"

He looked at her and nodded, but swayed as he made the motion. She picked him up, but he weighed too much for her to carry him on her hip like she used to, so she rotated him onto her back.

"Put your toes in my pockets, Frank. It will help me hold you."

He did as she ordered, laying his feverish head upon her shoulder and wrapped his arms around her neck. She left everything else behind, including Herman, who was still in the woods, and began to run home.

With Frank plastered against her back, she could hear and feel the rattling in his throat and chest. Oblivious to her own panicked breathing, she traveled as fast as possible over the rough terrain of the over-grown path. The force of Frank's feet in her pockets nearly pushed the loose-fitting trousers off her hips.

She heard crashing sounds behind them and realized Herman had given up his creature chase to catch up with them. He thought her running was a game and barked playfully.

She held onto Frank with both hands, which made her unable to knock the brush out of their way. She felt the stabs of shrubs and brambles on her face, neck and arms. Several times Frank wailed about the prickling, but she didn't dare slow down. While she struggled, she tried to recall anything and everything she knew about fevers, coughs, and illnesses.

He had run a temperature several times as a baby, but Mama always knew what to do to make him better. Jo remembered Mama bathed him in cool water, made poultices for his chest, and forced him to drink a lot of water and broth.

Somewhere in the house was a book where Mama had marked down her poultice mixtures for the family and what complaints they were used for. She didn't know where the book was, but vowed to find it.

Did she have time to go get some help for Frank? The only ride at the farm was Skeeter, and he'd be slow trying to carry both of them to the Pritchard farm. As sick as Frank was, she didn't dare leave him alone to get help. Her only logical choice was to get his fever down first, and then pack him to Mrs. Pritchard.

At their cabin, she kicked the door open and ran to Papa's bed, pouring Frank onto the covers like molasses. He seemed to be half-awake and half-asleep, producing a heavy rattle with every breath. She stripped off his shirt and trousers, covered him with quilts, then turned to do what little she knew about healing.

She ran to the barn to bring the bathing tub into the house. Herman ran behind her, barking with every step. Although she got a purchase on the tub, it was too heavy for her to shift alone. She scanned the barn and spotted a big round pan with handles Papa used for gardening. She grabbed it and ran to the well to fill it with water. She couldn't shift it full, so was forced to pour out half the water before she could carry it. Even half full, walking was difficult, and she sloshed water on her trousers and shirt with every step.

Inside, she set the pan down by the bed and gathered towels and smaller linens to drop into the water. She then wrung them out and wrapped Frank in their coolness.

He didn't take to her doing this, and began to fight her, coughing in protest.

"Leave 'em be!" she barked. She struggled to cap the urge to scream at him in fear. "You need these to quiet your fever!"

Once he followed her orders, she grabbed several pots, ran and filled them at the well, then started a fire in the cookstove. She knew steam might help his breathing.

She brought him a cup of cool water, shaking him awake enough to make him drink it. He looked like he wanted to cry and fight her about being forced to swallow, but he surrendered and downed the measure.

His towels were already warm, so she re-dipped them in the water bowl and prayed they'd do some good, as she swaddled him again. She touched his red cheeks and ran her fingertips through his hair. He was so sick. It happened so quickly.

An attempt to peer down his throat was unsuccessful. She lit an oil lamp and tried again. His throat was red, and swollen to boot.

She ruminated over his possible condition. He could have a touch of ague, but Tommy Marshfield was afflicted with that and it seemed a body had to fight that all the time. As she rotated the lamp, grayish-colored mucus could be seen on and around the back of his throat. When she saw it, she sucked in a big gulp of air.

Croup. It was croup that was making him cough and blocked his breathing. This fact horrified her. Tears welled in her eyes as she pushed the names of the people who had succumbed to croup out of her mind.

She had no choice but to shift the thick mucus from his throat before steam could help his breathing. After a frantic search of the cabinets, she found a packet of medicine Mama used to make her vomit when she'd eaten something bad several years ago. She brought the packet to the bedside lamp and inspected it. She placed the bitter powder on her tongue and was sure she'd found the medicine Frank needed.

The light of the lamp revealed the packet was only half full. She didn't have any idea how much he would need, but prayed there was enough to do the job. With so little available, she couldn't risk him fighting her, causing a spill.

She took the packet to the table, poured a small measure into a cup, added water and stirred it, then carried the cup back to Frank. She braced his head and forced the measure past his lips once his cough quieted down. His brown eyes widened with surprise as the bitter taste rolled into his mouth.

"You *must* drink this, Frank, *you must!*" Jo said with a voice she hoped matched Papa's when he was very angry. "It's awful, but *you must!*"

With a tearful whine, he complied.

When Mama had been brought down by pneumonia, Doc Collins tried his best to cure her, but her grave on the hill was a testament to his failure. She would never forget the sound of her mother's labored breathing, and it terrified her how similar Frank sounded. She put her arms around him and began humming a tune, unable to listen another second to his gasps for air.

Just for a brief moment, her mind's eye saw the image of a tiny cross at the top of the hill beside her mother's cross. Panic crawled upon her skin when she thought of him suffering Mama's fate. The sobs she'd previously been able to prevent now came pouring out of her like a stream after a spring storm.

How can I live with myself if I fail him? I've been so resentful about being left here with him, and now he might die.

She let go of Frank and got down on her knees.

I'm sorry, God. I swear I'll never resent him again. Please God, let him live. He's just a little boy.

She prayed until he began to retch. She captured his production in an empty pan through tear-filled eyes, pouring each delivery into the slop jar between waves. As she poured, she could see a little of the mucus had been shifted. *It was working*

When his retching came to a halt, the rattle was still audible. Giving him a short respite from the medicine, she replaced his warm towels with cool ones and made him drink more water.

When his rattle was louder, she forced him to swallow another measure of the medicine. He kicked and swung at her again, but finally, most of the bitter concoction was consumed.

Then, as before, she filled the waiting time with prayers.

At the end of his second round of vomiting, there was hardly any rattle to be heard. She exchanged his hot towels with cool replacements and scooted a small table to the edge of the bed near his face. She set the steaming kettle upon one folded, heavy tablecloth and made a tent from the kettle to his face with another.

The steam seemed to help him, so she kept it coming for a long time, replacing the contents of the kettle when the steam fell.

After some time, he rasped and coughed, but without the earlier wet rattles.

Sally bellowed from the barn and she realized the cow had walked herself there to be milked. Where had the day gone? She removed the steam tent and re-applied cool towels to Frank. Then she ran and milked Sally enough to ease her pressure, shooting the milk into a puddle, much to the cat's delight.

Back inside, the only action she hadn't tried yet was to make a poultice. But to do that, she needed to find Mama's book. She rummaged through every trunk, drawer and cupboard, heedless of the mess she made. She located it in Papa's nightstand. The sight of Mama's beautiful script on the pages gave her comfort, as if she reached down from heaven to help Frank.

She gathered the suggested ingredients for the poultice and mixed them. Frank didn't react when she placed the offensive-smelling mixture on his chest. Once again, she swaddled him in cool towels.

After this, she waited for the poultice to work and realized how tired she'd become. She lay across the end of the bed to rest her eyes for just a moment.

It was dark in the house when she heard him call.

"Jo?" his reedy voice trembled. A series of coughs overtook him.

"I'm here, Frank." She patted his leg and rose to snatch the lamp from the table to judge his condition.

When she returned, she ran her fingers across his clammy skin and noted there was less fever. Her heart raced.

"Are you feeling better?"

He nodded, almost lost in the feather pillow on Papa's bed. The circles around his eyes were still sunken, yet it seemed as if a spark of light had replaced his frightening dull stare.

"Don't like ya making me drink that med'sine, Jo."

She clutched his hand. "If you promise not to get sick anymore, I swear you'll never have to drink it again."

"You swear?"

"I do," she said, her voice filled with emotions he couldn't understand.

He fell asleep after she made him drink another cup of water. He didn't hear her tearful prayers of thanks to God and their mother.

One evening a week later, Herman began barking while Frank milked Sally.

"I'll finish, so you can see who's coming," she said with a smile.

215

He flashed a matching grin and raced from the barn.

She heard his squeal of delight, which propelled her to finish the task. Papa and Buck had returned.

They were a wonderful sight to see, tan from the sun and dusty from their ride, smiles painted their faces. The new horses trailed behind Clovis — a beautiful lot and plenty of them.

After Papa tossed Frank into the air and kissed him, he put an arm around her. "Have you forgiven me for leaving you with Frank and the chores?"

"You made the right decision to leave me here, Papa."

He knew there was a story behind her words.

She smiled at him. "You'll hear the whole story after Frank's asleep." Then she ran to give Buck a hug.

SOMEBODY ELSE'S GOLD

BY ANTHONY WOOD

Grandpa's dark oak casket divided the family at the front of the church, poised like two opposing armies. Two sets of pallbearers, still as statues, stood on each side in chaps with hats covering hands resting on pistols — ready to ride, ready to fight. Nobody moved. We all knew what it would lead to if someone did move. Suspicious eyes remained opened as Pastor Moore searched for an ending to his final prayer. He rambled aimlessly and grunted like a man straining in the outhouse. I peeked from underneath my mop of blonde hair to catch men watching each other from corners of their eyes. As Pastor Moore read Psalm 23, a heavy darkness shrouded Grandpa's passing over the Jordan River.

This was no celebration of a life well lived, no telling of old stories to make us laugh, no words of wisdom handed down for succeeding generations. Pastor Moore never even mentioned Grandpa's name for sticking to his canned sermon with highfalutin words most of us didn't understand. Grandpa wouldn't have cared. He didn't like Pastor Moore anyway, except that he preached what Grandpa told him. Besides, Grandpa didn't want any favors. Being preached into heaven would've been the last thing he'd want at his funeral. I don't believe Grandpa would've gone through the pearly gates if the preacher talked St. Peter into letting him in. Grandpa said he'd get in on his own, or cut cards for it.

The day was dark as the black clothes we wore in the dimly lit house of worship. Menacing clouds filled the sky, but there was no smell of rain in the air — just dry, dusty wind choking throats and blurring eyes. There'd be no dinner on the ground afterwards and no flowers planted on Grandpa's grave on this day of reckoning. I stood by Grandpa's casket wondering, What's fixin' to happen?

Grandpa finished his race — no more debts to settle, no more trouble to stir. But he hoped the feud he'd created between his twin sons, Jacob and Esau, would continue long after he was gone. I could almost hear him laughing. But there was no laughing that day.

Tension filled the church house like a bronc about to be ridden for the first time. All hell could break loose any second. I couldn't resist. I peered over into the ornately carved oak box with shiny brass handles. A deep furrow creased my grandpa's forehead. He ain't at peace, even now.

Grandpa pioneered this part of west Texas just after the Mexican War. He built a cattle spread the size of a small country out of the wilderness with his own two hands, boasting that the only thing the Lord did to help him was get in his way. Grandpa loved the Lord, but not his teachings.

Grandpa's very presence created greed. He even brought Pastor Moore from back East to become the family reverend in this church house on his land. Grandpa controlled the Lord's Word and the man who spoke it. Pastor Moore preached on the expectation of riches and blessing in this life from the Lord. He too had caught the greed disease, hoping he'd cash in on Grandpa's death somehow.

Grandpa expected nothing from anyone and gave nothing in return. He often crowed, "Ain't worth havin' if you can't have it all!" He lived by the philosophy I will take it with me when I go! Not literally, but through whichever son beat the other out of the inheritance. Grandpa was a simple man whose only guilty pleasure, besides the moonshine he made and hoarded for himself, was watching Jacob and Esau fuss and fight over who was Grandpa's favorite, meaning who'd get the ranch and the riches after he died.

When Pa and Uncle Esau were just boys, Grandpa made them work all week like everybody else. Come Saturday, he'd pay his hands wages owed. Not his sons. He'd circle the ranch hands in a ring, throw a week's pay in gold in the center, and let his sons fight over who'd get paid. Grandpa didn't teach Jacob and Esau to share, only to compete and let greed rule their souls.

The sun was going down and Pastor Moore looked up from his Bible. He could delay the inevitable no longer. "And I will dwell in the house of the Lord forever, amen."

That final amen prompted the fight that would bring the feud to a head. There surely was no goodness or mercy following this bunch. Both sides of the family wanted to care for the casket because both knew what was in Grandpa's vest pocket. Both offered to dig the grave and lower the box because both wanted to sneak the legal parchment holding the entirety of Grandpa's wealth.

Both wanted Grandpa covered up quickly to cash in on his riches.

Uncle Esau stepped forward. "Me and mine'll take the casket in the wagon up the hill. Don't need your help."

Pa barked, "The hell you say! We're takin' it!"

Both sides threatened the other with coats pulled back and side arms gleaming. Pastor Moore stood between them with his only weapons — Scripture and prayer. But that power was lost long ago to his not-so-secret sin. He stepped back, just as likely to get shot for his interest in Grandpa's fortune as anyone in the room.

Before he died, Grandpa converted ownership of his railroad stock, land holdings, cattle herd, and even his ranch house into a will that guaranteed ownership to whomever presented the legal document to his lawyer. One page of parchment held the wealth of the world for this family — easy to grab, simple to cash, and certainly didn't carry the weight of the gold it represented. That burden would be for the presenter of the document to bear and it'd take a wagon to carry it away. Grandpa set it up that way to ensure his legacy of greed continued. And that a fight would decide ownership and his sons forever would hate each other. Pastor

Moore held out his arms to keep the opposing sides at bay. His cross-like posture
brought no healing.

"Yea, though I walk through the valley of
death, I will fear no evil." Pastor Moore's
words meant nothing to men whose hackles
stood on end. He discreetly searched for a
place to hide, fearing the evil in this house
of peace. I spied a spot under Grandpa's
casket.

Twilight stole the daylight and coal oil
lamps were lit. No amount of Pastor
Moore's persuading convinced either twin
to compromise. This truly was a story
straight from the Good Book, except there
was nothing good in this. Then the wrong
words came from the wrong mouth.

Uncle Esau snickered, "Pa always thought
you were too weak to run the ranch, boy."

My Pa replied, skinning his Colt .44
quicker'n a rattler strike.

Pastor Moore dove behind his pulpit.

Guns blazed, women screamed, and children ducked. The casket flipped over, spilling Grandpa out and knocking me to the
floor. A lamp broke and coal oil spilled in
every direction, making the floor slippery as
greased glass. Flames leaped across the
room and the smell of pine resin thickened
in the blinding black smoke. The crowd

fought tooth and nail to get out with no regard for young children and old people. Pistols ceased and knives were sheathed. Like cattle herded into a holding pen, they pushed and shoved to get out like Grandpa taught — every person for himself.

Pa and Uncle Esau hesitated. For a second, I thought they'd become brothers again. Uncle Esau reared back to punch my pa in the jaw. Pa ducked and head-butted his brother in the stomach. I watched the struggle as flames singed my hair and scorched my clothes. I didn't know what to do.

Then I saw them — Grandpa's eyes drawn open, blankly staring at me. His evil grin sent chills through my body like somebody had poured ice water down my back.

Then I saw it — the source of this worthless feud. I snatched the document out of Grandpa's coat pocket and stuffed it in my shirt. I looked back. Grandpa's eyes had closed and his smile relaxed. I shuddered like big spiders were crawling all over me.

Then I saw Pa and Uncle Esau locked in a wrestler's hold but with eyes glued on me. Neither could speak for choking on smoke. Neither could move for the grip each had on the other. But they saw I had the paper containing the wealth of a lifetime. I didn't know what to do, but they did. They tussled around on the burning floor like two kids kicking ashes and cinders from smoldering chunks of wood. Spilled coal oil soaked their clothes and burst into flames. Both screamed like mountain lions but kept up the fight to get to me and the document.

Crash! Rafters and roofing fell in a fiery smash. I didn't want to look, but I did. Jacob and Esau were dead. Twin brothers killed for a birthright neither would ever enjoy. Suddenly the flames found a stream of coal oil that slithered toward me like a fiery serpent. I'm a goner!

I pulled the half opened casket over me, leaving a small crack for air. The heat was unbearable, but there was nowhere else to go. I spied Grandpa just outside the casket turning black. I screamed, "You left me no way out of all this!"

Crack, smash, thud! More charred rafters landed on church pews and the casket. I didn't know if it was fear or the choking smoke that took the breath from me. I covered my mouth with the handkerchief my mother made me carry to church. My eyes burned and my chest ached. My nose bled and my pants smoked. My hair withered and my ears burned. I couldn't breathe. Am I gonna die?

Then everything went dark.

A burst of dawn sunlight blinded me and I yelled, "Heaven?" According to Pastor Moore, you could never know until you died. Am I dead? Voices called out searchingly. Are they angel voices or demons? In this place, it could be either.

Pastor Moore heckled, "No, son, this ain't heaven. But of anyone here, you'd be the first to go." His words rasped across my blistered ears, "Are you alright?" With Pastor Moore asking, I wasn't sure of anything. "Just hold on a bit. They're comin' to get you." He didn't want to blacken his hands to free me from the charred rafters piled on the casket. I guess his hands were dirty enough already.

He squatted down, careful not to let his pants touch the burnt wood. His gold chain sparkled in the dawning sunlight. His nickel plated pepperbox pistol wiggled inside his vest as he reached for my hand. I turned away. Grandpa lay next to me, his wicked half smile returned. Pa and Uncle Esau lay charred like used up charcoal.

I looked back at the gleaming gold watch chain. Pastor Moore reached to take my hand again. I shook my head. A thousand memories flooded my mind — the fights, the hateful gossip, the fake religion, the threats, the ruination of all things good in our family. Then I remembered. The parchment!

Pastor Moore smiled like Satan as I pulled from inside my shirt the document that contained legal ownership of everything Grandpa had accumulated on this earth and the source of all things evil in our family. He knew well the value of what I held in my hand.

Pastor Moore's whisper crackled like the burning of a thousand timbers. "You can have it all. I will help you, son." For a second, I thought I saw devil horns.

I clutched the paper close to my chest. Pastor Moore squinted, pondering my intentions. From the corner of my eye, I caught the flicker of a small flame behind me. Pastor Moore's eyes bulged like when he preached hellfire and damnation. He snatched, but I was quicker. He growled like a demon crawling out of Hell, until the left side of the smoldering church house wall creaked as it swiftly caved over. Pastor Moore stood straight up to watch it fall, but not before he turned to me with the eyes of a man who knew he had only seconds to live.

"Purgatory for all my sins, Father, please . . ."

Whoosh! Pastor Moore was no more.

The breath of the falling wall snuffed out the remaining flames. The casket pinned me even tighter against the hard pine floor. Trapped, I cradled the document against my chest.

"Anybody here?"

I reached my slightly burned hand out to pat the ashes. Immediately boards were shoved aside, and the casket was carefully raised. Hands pulled me by the shoulders from underneath the charred oak box. I'm alive!

"You alright, Cousin Abel? Just know'd you was dead!" I breathed in fresh air that stank of burnt flesh. I shook the ashes from my clothes and dusted my hair. Except for a few burns and scrapes, I was fine.

"Better now that I see your ugly catfish face, Cousin Cain! Thanks for rescuin' me."

"Don't mention it, frog head." We stumbled over the remains of our fathers and their church to sit on the front steps. We didn't look back.

Men sifted through the ashes and burnt wood to find Grandpa, Uncle Esau, and my pa, Jacob. I didn't want to look, but I had to — nothing but ashes and bones of lives gone. Ashes to ashes. Hmmph, bet Pastor Moore has a new understanding of that verse. They left the preacher where he lay. I guess he needs a little hellfire and damnation before they pull his carcass out.

Cain handed me a dipper of water. I drank half to cool my parched throat and splashed my face with the rest to wash off the smoky darkness of Hell. When no one was looking, I pulled out the legal document that held the wealth of our world. Cain snatched it so no one could see.

"Do you realize what you got here?" I nodded. For two boys whose fathers hated each other, Cain and I had been best friends since we both could remember.

Cain grinned and winked. "You thinkin' what I'm thinkin'?"

We each took a corner of the legal document that possessed the wealth of our small world and held it over a small flickering flame in the dry grass by the church house steps. The parchment went up in smoke, and with it, the gold of somebody else's world. Cain picked a weed to chew on and leaned back on the steps.

"Cousin Abel, what'll happen to Grandpa's railroad stock, bank money, cattle, and ranch now that he's gone?" I put my arm around his shoulder.

"Well, Cousin Cain, I guess we'll just have to share."

■ ■ ■ ■

"Somebody Else's Gold" was published in the Winter 2019 issue of *Saddlebag Dispatches*.

STRANGLEHOLD

BY GARY L. BREEZEEL

"Whoa!" Boone Cooper pulled back hard on Thunder's reins. Who'd blocked the bridge over Grizzly Gorge? With the only road closed off, how would he reach Silverton?

He dismounted, strode over, and lifted the barricade.

"Drop that gate!" A man sauntered out from behind a rock beyond the gorge, his right hand poised above the six-gun worn low on his hip. Dressed in black from head to toe, he was tall and lean, his steel-gray eyes cold and dead. A sure sign of a remorseless killer. "I said drop it. Before I drop you."

Boone let the bar fall into place. "What's going on here? This is a public road."

The gunman stopped in the middle of the bridge. "It's a toll bridge now. Nobody crosses without paying. 'Specially, the likes of you. I ain't got no use for lowdown

Confederates. That gray uniform brands you as a lily-livered back shooter. Now pay up — two dollars for a man on horseback — or git."

"I don't have any money, but I need to get into town."

"Well, you've got a six-gun on your hip, Johnny Reb. If you wanna cross, draw."

Boone glowered but turned away.

"I knew you were yellow. Like all your kind."

Boone glanced back.

"On second thought, I think I'll shoot you just to rid the world of a mangy varmint." The gatekeeper went for his gun.

Boone whirled, drew, and pulled the trigger.

The other man's six-shooter tumbled into the gorge. He grabbed his shoulder. "You should've finished me when you had the chance. I'll get you for this if it's the last thing I do."

"The war's over. I've had enough of killing. Do yourself a favor and find another line of work." Boone lifted the gate, mounted Thunder, and rode off down the road. With luck, he'd never encounter that polecat again.

Boone tied his horse to the hitching post

and clomped across the boardwalk into Cooper's Mercantile. "Can a fella get some service in here?"

Behind the counter, a man with thinning gray hair did a double-take. "Boone! You're home!" He rushed to Boone and threw his arms around him. "I've prayed for this day for four years."

"Me, too, Dad. I'm delighted to see you." He scanned the store where he'd grown up. His chest tightened. "Why the almost bare shelves?"

"I'll explain, but first, let's get you out of that grubby uniform. Although things are kinda sparse, I think we can outfit you."

An hour later, bathed and dressed in clean clothes for the first time in months, Boone took a seat at the table across from his father. "Everything smells great. It's good to be home, even though the place seems empty without Mama."

"It's been a long year. Since you didn't look for her, I take it you got my letter?" Dad handed him a plate of biscuits.

Boone nodded as he helped himself to a slice of ham and a sizable helping of fried potatoes. "While I eat, why don't you tell me about the bare shelves?"

"Two years ago, Grover Osbourne moved into Silverton and took over. He's slick.

First, he bought the saloon. A couple of months later, he grabbed the Bonanza Mine. Brought in a bunch of gunslingers to impose his will. Now, he has us in a stranglehold."

"I had a run-in with one of his men at Grizzly Gorge. He won't pull his gun on anybody for a spell."

"I wondered how you got into town." Dad sipped his coffee. "Anyone who opposes Osbourne winds up dead. Somebody drygulched the town marshal. Now, nobody'll take the job. Three months back, the sidewinder opened a general store down the street. Six weeks ago, his toadies on the city council imposed outrageous tolls to cross the bridge. A thousand dollars per freight wagon. All to run me out of business. I can't restock. My customers have deserted me. They have no choice but to pay his sky-high prices."

"Don't worry. I'm here now. I'll find a way to outwit Osbourne and bring in the supplies you need."

As Boone restocked shelves, he listened to the hubbub of the shoppers who filled the mercantile. What a pleasant change from his arrival two weeks earlier.

He set the last can in place and joined his

father behind the counter. "Looks like your shoppers have come back."

"It's wonderful to have the store crowded again. I can't thank you enough. I'd never have thought to use mules and carry merchandise over the old Indian trail through the mountains."

A woman stepped up and set a full basket on the countertop.

Dad smiled. "Good morning, Mrs. Schwartz. Did you find everything you need?"

"Yes, except for Papa's pipe tobacco."

He reached behind him and added a tin to her items. "That'll be three dollars. Shall I add it to your account?"

She nodded. "Thank you, Mr. Cooper."

Several others made purchases over the next twenty minutes.

When the last customer left, his father closed and locked the door. "I'm glad to have all this business, but Osbourne won't take it lying down."

"Yeah, he'll retaliate, somehow. I'll keep an eye out. Starting tonight."

"Let's leave everything for now. It's been a long day. I can straighten up in the morning." Dad led the way to the living quarters upstairs. "Let's rest awhile before we fix supper."

"Suits me." Boone sat in Mama's rocker across from Dad's wingback chair. "Have you heard from that brother of mine lately?"

"Got a letter last week. Henry found a job at a bank in San Francisco, and his wife's expecting again, their third."

"I'm glad he's doing well." For several minutes, the only sounds were the creaks as he rocked and the ticking of the clock on the mantel.

After a while, his father broke the silence. "The way things are going, we'll need a new shipment before the week's out. I'm not sure six mules will be enough."

"Maybe I can buy a couple more."

"Oh, I forgot to tell you. Doc patched up Montana the best he could, but word's gotten around that your bullet shattered his shoulder joint. That gunslinger will never draw a gun again. Still, he'll want revenge. Watch your back, Son."

At eleven o'clock that night, Boone slipped out the back door and took a position in the shadows beside the storage shed.

Hours later, a figure crept around the corner of the building next door and approached the rear of the store. The moonlight revealed a bulky object in the man's hand.

Boone stepped out and cocked his six-shooter with an audible click. "Stop right there. Reach for the sky."

The man set the item down, tossed his gun away, and raised his hands.

Boone pressed the barrel of his Colt against his captive's belly, struck a match, and held it near the other's face. An Osbourne lackey.

Boone blew out the match. "What do we have here?" Keeping the six-gun in place, he bent over and unscrewed the can's lid. An odor of kerosene filled the air. "Mighty suspicious behavior, if you ask me. Let's go pay a visit to your boss." He stepped behind the man and marched him around the store and across the street to Osbourne's saloon.

Once in the establishment, he opened the office door without knocking and shoved the would-be arsonist inside.

Seated at his desk, Osbourne jumped to his feet. "What's the meaning of this?"

Boone marched into the room. "I caught your hired hand trying to burn down Dad's store."

Open-mouthed, Osbourne stared at his employee. "Smiley, is this true?"

"No, sir. I was on my way out to the ranch."

Boone thrust his hands onto his hips. "On

foot? In back of the mercantile? With a container of kerosene? Nice try. But I don't buy it. Osbourne, the next varmint I return to you won't be in such good shape. You'd better keep them in hand."

The forty-mile trip from Virginia City had been uneventful, so far. Yet, Boone needed to remain vigilant as he drew nearer to Silverton. He glanced over his shoulder at the eight heavily-laden mules who followed him. Ahead lay Paiute Pass, a perfect place for an ambush.

His eyes darted from one rim to the other. Nothing moved.

About halfway through, a gunshot kicked up dust inches from Thunder's feet. Boone spurred the stallion into a gallop. Additional shots resounded as they sped out of harm's way.

Once outside the pass, he secured Thunder and the pack mules in a gully off the trail, then dismounted. He crept up the steep grade toward where the gunshots must have come from.

As he neared the top, a bullet whizzed past his ear. He flattened himself on the ground. The next shot knocked his hat off. He snaked his way to a nearby boulder. Under its cover, he stood, pulled his gun, and peeked around. Montana crouched behind a Utah juniper with a rifle pointed straight at Boone.

He ducked as his would-be assassin fired. The slug ricocheted off the rockface beside where Boone's head had been.

After a moment, he peeped out and snapped a quick shot in the gunman's direction. Then, he tiptoed past his boulder, belly-crawled to a patch of sage, circled a rock formation, and slipped up behind his assailant. "Okay, Montana, drop it."

The bushwhacker turned his head but, otherwise, remained still.

"Throw away the gun. Don't make me kill you."

The badman whirled, rifle pointed toward Boone. As Boone fired, smoke drifted from his gun barrel. Montana crumpled, hands clutching his abdomen. His weapon dropped to the ground.

Boone knelt next to him. "You're done for. Gut shot. Why not make a clean breast of things before you die? Who sent you after me?"

The wounded man grimaced. "Osbourne . . . put . . . five-hundred-dollar . . . bounty on your head. Another five hundred . . . to capture . . . shipment."

"Who killed the marshal?"

"Blacksnake. I was there . . . when Osbourne . . . paid him off. Two hundred." Montana fixed his gaze on Boone. "Please. Finish me. Don't let me suffer."

"I can't kill a man in cold blood, even to spare him pain." He rose, turned, and walked away.

As he mounted Thunder, a gunshot rang out.

A silver star on his chest, Boone flung open the door to Osbourne's office in the saloon and strode inside.

From his seat behind the desk, the villain-in-chief looked up. His jaw dropped and his head snapped back. "Cooper!"

"Surprised to see me? Your errand boy failed at his mission. I'm still alive."

Osborne squinted. "I have no idea what you're talking about."

"Save your breath. Montana talked before he died. I twisted the arm of your friend, the mayor, and got him to appoint me marshal. You're under arrest. For the murder of Marshal Willard, among other things."

Osbourne jumped to his feet. "I didn't kill him."

"No, but you hired the man who did. Montana spilled the beans. Come on. Time to join Blacksnake in the calaboose."

"Very well. I'll go with you." He circled around the desk. "But I'll be free before you know it. I have the best lawyers in the territory on my payroll."

"We'll see about that."

"Just let me get my hat." The outlaw leader reached toward the hat rack, swirled, and socked Boone on the jaw. Knocked off balance, he stumbled and fell to the floor.

Must be going soft. How had he fallen for such a sucker play? Should have known the arrest had gone too easy.

Osbourne leaped on Boone and grasped his throat.

He boxed the villain's ears. The other's grip loosened. With a mighty shove, Boone knocked his attacker off to one side and scrambled to his feet. Now, it was a fair fight.

Head lowered, the saloonkeeper charged. Boone sidestepped and slammed him head-first into the wall. Osbourne staggered, recovered, pivoted, and kicked Boone in the groin. Then, he dashed to the desk and pulled open a top drawer. When he straightened, he held a gun.

Boone drew and fired.

Osbourne jerked. His gaze drifted down to the crimson stain spreading across his chest. Seconds later, his eyes glazed over. He wilted and fell onto the desk.

At the sound of the gunshot, three of Osbourne's hired guns rushed in.

Boone kept his Colt at the ready. "I'm the new marshal. Your boss is dead. If you know what's good for you, you'll hightail it out of town."

All three dashed through the open door.

Boone smiled. He'd broken the stranglehold on Silverton.

ABOUT THE AUTHORS

Gary L. Breezeel began his first novel in 1964. That blight on the literary world remains unfinished to the everlasting benefit of readers everywhere. However, he has completed drafts of two Christian romance novels. Neither is ready for publication. A member of American Christian Fiction Writers, he has written short stories in various genres, including mystery, romance, fantasy, and horror. He has won numerous contests including Del Garrett's Gimme the Creeps Contest, White County Creative Writers' Contest, and Del Garrett's Triple Scoop Writing Contest. A native of Southeast Missouri, Gary now lives in Searcy, Arkansas.

Del Garrett is an Arkansas Hall of Fame writer, and the author of six novels: *Texas Justice, While the Angels Slept, Shadow-light, The Buccaneer's Daughter, The El Dorado*

Trail, and Whispers in the Wind — The Search for Jack the Ripper, a crime novella series featuring private detective Felix Nash, plus an anthology of short stories he calls *Del Garrett's Flea Market Tales.* Del's first attempt at writing fiction, a Civil War short story, was published by *Louis L'Amour Western Magazine.* He has also been published in *Pro Se Productions, Blood Moon Rising, Gateway Science Fiction* and *Storyteller Magazine.* He won an international award for Best Historical Western Fiction and numerous other contest awards. His poetry has been published by the Missouri Poetry Society. He is a former radio and TV announcer. He owns Raven's Inn Press which publishes fiction and nonfiction books and anthologies.

Don Money was born and raised on a small Arkansas farm. His interest in writing began in the sixth grade when he wrote his first short story as a Gifted and Talented project. After graduation, he joined the US Air Force and traveled the globe as a Nuclear, Biological, Chemical Weapons Defense Specialist. After ten years in the service, he returned to his roots in Arkansas and now teaches Language Arts to sixth graders at Beebe Middle School. Don has short stories published in a variety of anthologies, including *The Vault of Terror, Trembling With Fear, Shacklebound Books, Black Hare Press,* and *Medusa Tales* magazine. His stories have won contests at the White County Creative Writers Conference, the Arkansas Writers Conference, and Ozark Creative Writers Conference. Don can be found on Twitter @donmoney-writing.

Rhonda Roberts writes short stories, poetry, essays and memoirs. In the last few years, she has focused primarily on writing for children. Rhonda has been married to her best friend for 43 years, has two children and three cats. She has won several local, state, and national awards, most notably the 2008 Highlights for Children's Annual Fiction Contest. She has been twice honored as Author of the Month for Highlights.

Gary Rodgers grew up in rural Arkansas in an age when children learned to be seen and not heard. As a result, he inherited the art of tall tales and lively storytelling at the feet of his grandparents and many uncles, aunts, and cousins. After a tour in the Army, then a job which took him to all fifty states, all provinces of Canada, and Jamaica, he retired to his rural Arkansas roots. Gary lives with his wife, writer Kimberly Vernon, and an assortment of rescue pets. Gary's stories have appeared in *Saddlebag Dispatches* magazine and several local and regional anthologies.

Kimberly Vernon has won many local and regional awards for her short stories, poetry, and essays. Her work has appeared in several anthologies and magazines. She writes a monthly non-fiction feature for *Life in Chenal Magazine.* She has published a collection of poetry, *A Rhyme for Every Season,* and a children's book, *Toolshed Surprise.* Kim lives in central Arkansas with her husband, award-winning writer Gary Rodgers. The couple share their home with three rescued pets. The two enjoy traveling, reading, and competing in writing contests. Her website is www.kimberlyvernon.net[1].

Ellen Withers is an award-winning fiction writer, freelance writer, and retired insurance fraud investigator. Her mystery dual-time series, Show Me Mysteries, set in her picturesque hometown of Mexico, Missouri, is published by Scrivenings Press. *Show Me Betrayal,* was published May 2023 and

1. http://www.kimberlyvernon.net

Show Me Deceit, will publish May 2024. A nonfiction book to help writers win writing contests is scheduled March 2024 by Scrivenings Press titled, Magic Words: Enchant Judges & Conjure Contest Wins for Novels, Short Fiction, and Nonfiction. More information about Ellen, her books, writing tips, and highlights of guest authors is on her website: www.ellenewithers.com.

Anthony Wood grew up in historic Natchez, Mississippi, fueling a lifelong love of history. He is the author of A Tale of Two Colors, a series of Civil War-era historical novels based on the real-life wartime journey of his ancestor, Columbus "Lummy" Nathan Tullos. His writing has won a number of awards, including a Will Rogers Medallion for his Western short story "Not So Long in the Tooth." He serves as President of White County Creative Writers and as Managing Editor of *Saddlebag Dispatches* western magazine. Find more information about Anthony at www.anthony woodauthor.com[2].

2. http://www.anthonywoodauthor.com

Printed in the USA
CPSIA information can be obtained
at www.ICGtesting.com
JSHW080140070624
64343JS00009B/10